CATE TIERNAN

SEEKER

The tenth book in the series

PUFFIN BOOKS

Published by the Penguin Group
Penguin Books Ltd, 80 Strand, London WC2R 0RL, England
Penguin Putnam Inc., 375 Hudson Street, New York, New York 10014, USA
Penguin Books Australia Ltd, 250 Camberwell Road, Camberwell, Victoria 3124, Australia
Penguin Books Canada Ltd, 10 Alcorn Avenue, Toronto, Ontario, Canada M4V 3B2
Penguin Books India (P) Ltd, 11 Community Centre, Panchsheel Park, New Delhi – 110 017, India
Penguin Books (NZ) Ltd, Cnr Rosedale and Airborne Roads, Albany, Auckland, New Zealand
Penguin Books (South Africa) (Pty) Ltd, 24 Sturdee Avenue, Rosebank 2196, South Africa

Penguin Books Ltd, Registered Offices: 80 Strand, London WC2R 0RL, England

www.penguin.com

First published in the USA in Puffin Books,
a division of Penguin Putnam Books for Young Readers, 2002
Published in Great Britain in Puffin Books 2002

1

Printed in England by Clays Ltd, St Ives plc

British Library Cataloguing in Publication Data
A CIP catalogue record for this book is available from the British Library

ISBN 0–141–31551–2

To my three nephews:
Paul, Daniel and Coltrane.

1.
Invitation

Poor Dagda is still clomping around the house in his kitty cast. He has another week before it can come off. In the meantime he keeps giving me baleful stares, as if it were my fault that he ran in front of that car.

Since Hunter dropped the bomb about Sky's lead on his parents, I've been waiting for him to say, "Today's the day—I'm off." But he hasn't yet. Hunter. He makes me crazy; he keeps me sane. He seems so—English sometimes, kind of distant or reserved, but then he'll look at me, and his eyes see right through to my soul, and I go all shivery and want to kiss him. He makes me feel safe, and at the same time he makes me feel like I'm standing on the edge of a cliff. Does love always feel like this?

—Morgan

Since Sky's been gone, I'm amazed by what her presence meant in this house. There's less laundry. There's more food, but of a less interesting kind. The post is piling up—why does she get so many bloody catalogs? I always get the good parking spot right in front of the walkway. And the house is quiet: there are no vibrations that tell me I'm not alone, that my cousin is with me.

Now I'm here, and there's no getting around it—male laundry is boring. I wear jeans and shirts and socks and underwear. Those four things, day and night, summer and winter. Sky's clothes are so much more complicated—all sorts of weird girl-type articles of clothing, things I couldn't even name. Morgan doesn't seem to have as many varieties of clothes as Sky. She mostly wears corduroys or jeans, shirts or sweatshirts. Plain underwear, no bra, ever. (Excellent.) It's funny—she doesn't ever deliberately try to be sexy. She doesn't have to. Just looking at her, in her regular clothes, and knowing what she feels like wrapped around me, pressed hard against me, knowing what her skin feels like, knowing the scent of her, the vibration of her, her aura . . . my brain cells start fusing, and I cease being able to form coherent sentences. Like right now.

I still can't get over Sky finding a lead on my parents. Seeing them again is something I've dreamed of for more than half my life. And now that my employer, The International Council of Witches, has given me permission and helped narrow down their whereabouts, I'm ready to go. I just need to make plans.

Alwyn, who was only four when they left, can barely remember them. Linden died trying to see them again. He failed. In some ways, it seems too huge. In the years they've been gone, my parents have taken on almost mythical proportions—witches say their names with reverence or curiosity or even disdain; they look at me as though their legacy was stamped on my forehead.

This is simultaneously the most exciting and most terrifying thing that has ever happened to me. More, even, than our run-in with Ciaran in New York. Or when Morgan shape-shifted into a wolf, tracked me, and almost ripped me apart. Goddess, what we've been through together. . . . I just wish Morgan could go with me now.

If Sky were here, she would offer to go. I wouldn't let her, though. She is still fairly battered emotionally from her breakup with Raven. Spending time in France will be good for her.

But to have Morgan by my side as I see my parents for the first time in over a decade would make this so much easier. She is practical, powerful, able to face almost anything. I need her so much.

Morgan met me at Practical Magick, one of the area's only occult bookstores. It was a popular Wiccan hangout, and I was good friends with the owner, Alyce Fernbrake. The bells over the door jangled, and I looked up to see Morgan coming toward me, a little smile on her face.

I'm over six feet, so I'm used to looking down at people, but Morgan always seems to be eye to eye with me. Objectively speaking, though, she's about seven inches shorter than me, which still makes her taller than a lot of women. At seventeen, Morgan's face shows no lines of age or wisdom, pain or laughter. Only striking bones, features that seem strong and womanly and intensely attractive. Her eyes are almost frighteningly knowledgeable, her expression solemn, her mouth generous yet not prone to vacuous smiles or asinine giggles. She is one of the most stubborn, strong willed, prickly, reserved, and irritating people I have ever met. I love her so much, my knees buckle every time she's near.

"Hi," she said.

"Hi. Let's go in the back."

Morgan and I passed through the tattered orange curtain that separates the back room from the rest of the shop. It fell closed behind us, and then we were standing, looking at each other in the poorly lit room.

Her hair was loose and needed brushing. It fell in unsmooth waves past her elbows, almost to her waist. Her black peacoat was unbuttoned; her jeans flared slightly, with thready bottoms, to the tops of her scuffed leather clogs. Her large, brownish-green eyes watched me, and her strong, classic nose was faintly pink from cold. This was Morgan Rowlands. The daughter of Maeve Riordan, the last, powerful witch of Belwicket, and of Ciaran MacEwan, who was one of the darkest Woodbanes that Wicca had ever known. Adopted daughter of Sean and Mary Grace Rowlands. My love.

My desire for her came with no warning, like a snake striking, and suddenly I pulled her to me by her jacket, pushing my hands beneath the heavy coat and around her back, feeling the sweater she wore. I had a brief glimpse of her startled, uptilted eyes before I closed my own and slanted my mouth across hers, kissing her with an urgency that both scared and embarrassed me.

But Morgan met fire with fire; she has never backed down from anything in the months I have known her, and she didn't push me away with false modesty now. Instead she clung to me, her arms moving around my waist, and kissed me back, hard, stepping closer to me and putting her feet between mine.

Finally, who knew how long later, we eased apart. I was

breathing hard, every muscle in my body tense and wired and urging me forward. Morgan's lips were red and soft; her eyes were searching mine.

"I missed you," I said, surprised to hear my voice sounding hoarse and breathless. She nodded, her own breath coming quick and shallow. "Come on, sit." I led her toward the battered wooden table, and we both sank onto chairs as if we had just finished a marathon. Every bit of idle chitchat I could have summoned fled my brain, and instead I just held her hand tightly and blurted out my news.

"I'm leaving Saturday for Canada, to see my parents."

Morgan's dark brown eyes widened, and for a moment she looked afraid. But that impression faded instantly, and I wasn't sure if I had really seen it.

She nodded. "I've been expecting this."

I gave a short laugh. "Yeah. The council contacted me again this morning. They actually gave me directions to my parents' *house*. Can you believe that? They think Mum and Da moved about three months ago."

She nodded thoughtfully, not meeting my eyes.

"I'm driving," I told her. "I think it'll take about eleven hours. They live in a little town north of Quebec City. Morgan— will you go with me?"

Surprise lit her eyes, almost immediately replaced by clear longing.

"I don't know how long I'll be gone," I said quickly. "But if you need to get back before I do, I can put you on a plane or train or rent you a car."

As we held hands across the little table, we both pictured what it would mean. Long, intimate conversations in the car.

Hours and hours of time alone together. Being together day and night. Meeting my parents, her being with me during this incredibly meaningful experience. It would take our relationship to a whole new level. I wanted her to say yes so badly.

"I want to go," she said slowly. "I really want to go." She fell silent again. In her mind, she was probably having an imaginary conversation with her parents. I groaned to myself. What had I been thinking? Her parents don't even allow boys in the house. There was no way they'd let their daughter take off to Canada without at least one chaperon, like we'd had in New York. And this would be a much bigger trip.

Her face fell, and I could feel her disappointment because it was mirrored by mine.

"I can't," she said. "Why am I even thinking about it? I'm still trying to get my grades out of the toilet, my parents are still twitchy around the edges, there's no school vacation anytime soon—it's impossible." Her voice held frustration and impatience.

"It's all right," I said, covering her hand with both of mine. "It's all right. I just thought I'd throw the idea out there. Don't worry about it. There will be plenty of time for us to take trips in the future."

She nodded, unconvinced, and I felt sorry for bringing the subject up; sorry for making her feel guilty that she couldn't accompany me on this important journey. Looking into her face, I brought her palm to my mouth and kissed it. She sighed, and I watched the heat flare in her eyes.

2.
Preparation

Goddess, I feel stupid. Stupid and childish and mad and guilty about not being able to go to Canada with Hunter. Why am I only seventeen? After what I've been through in the last five months, you'd think I would be at least twenty-three by now. I can't stand being my age. I want to live in my own place, make all my own decisions, study the craft as much and as openly as I'd like. I want to be an adult. I should be an adult. Until I discovered Wicca, I'd always assumed I'd finish high school, go to college, and get a job that was incredibly satisfying, fun, creative, and that paid a ton of money.

Now the whole rest of my life seems up in the air. Eoife wants me to go to Scotland to study with some important teachers. I want to be with Hunter. My parents expect me to go to college. What for? I have to take the SATs this spring, have to *start collecting college brochures. Suddenly everything seems so pointless.*

Oh, Hunter, how long will you be gone?

—Morgan

Alyce Fernbrake recommended a friend of hers, Bethany Malone, as someone to lead my coven, Kithic, while I was gone. When I rang her doorbell on Thursday night, I had no idea what to expect and wondered if my being a Seeker would have a negative effect on our meeting.

She opened the door almost immediately. As soon as I saw her, I realized that I had seen her at least a couple of times at various witch gatherings here and there. Bethany was almost as tall as I am, big boned, with large, strong hands and a sturdy-looking body. Her short black hair was fine and straight; her eyes were huge and so dark, they seemed to have no pupils. I guessed her age to be about forty-five.

"Hunter Niall," she said, looking at me consideringly. "Come in."

"Bethany," I greeted her. "Thanks for agreeing to see me."

She led me through the short foyer into her lounge. Despite the building's boxy, modern appearance, Bethany had created her own haven here, and this room was warm and felt familiar.

"I'm having some wine," she said, getting down a glass. "Will you have some?"

"Yes, thank you," I said, watching her pour the dark, rich fluid. I took the glass and looked into it, inhaling the scents of fruit, tannins, earth, and sun. I drank.

"This is terrific," I said, and she smiled and nodded. We

sat across from each other, me on the sofa and Bethany in a large, overstuffed chair that was draped with a mohair throw. The room was lit by shaded lamps and several candles; there were herbs hanging in neat rows along one wall. I sipped my wine and felt a bit of the day's tension start to melt away.

"Alyce told me you're looking for someone to lead your circles for a while," she said.

"Yes. I'm going out of town. Kithic is a fairly new coven, and I'd hate for them to get out of rhythm while I'm gone."

"Tell me about them," she said, folding her long legs beneath her. "Are you all one clan? I'm Brightendale—did Alyce mention it?"

"Yes, she did, and no, we aren't," I said. "In fact, out of the twelve, only three are blood witches—me, my cousin Sky, and a girl named Morgan Rowlands. And Sky's on holiday right now, so there would be only eleven, including you."

"Morgan Rowlands," said Bethany. "Goodness. She's in your coven? What's that like?"

I grimaced. "Unpredictable. Exciting. Frightening."

Nodding, Bethany swirled the wine in her glass. "What about the rest of them?"

"They're all in high school," I explained. "They've all known each other, more or less, for most of their lives. Widow's Vale is a pretty insular town, and there aren't many different schools. One girl, Alisa Soto, left the coven recently, but I have a feeling she'll be coming back. She was the youngest, at fifteen. The others are Bree Warren, Robbie Gurevitch, Sharon Goodfine, and Ethan Sharp. They're all juniors. Simon Bakehouse, Matt Adler, Thalia Cutter, Raven Meltzer, and Jenna Ruiz are all seniors."

"So many young people, coming to Wicca," said Bethany. "That's really nice. How sincere do they seem? Are they just flirting with it, or do you think they take it seriously?"

"Both," I said. "Some are more sincere than others. Some are more sincere than they realize. Some are less sincere than they realize. I'll leave it up to you to figure it out—I don't want to prejudice you."

Bethany nodded and sipped her wine. "Tell me about Morgan."

I paused for a few moments. How to put this? "Well, she's powerful," I said lamely. "She grew up in a Catholic family. She only started studying Wicca five months ago—and only found out about being a blood witch maybe four months ago. And she was, you know, involved with Selene Belltower and her son."

I tried to keep my face neutral as I said this. Cal hadn't been dead long enough. Anytime I thought of Cal and Morgan together, of him convincing her he loved her, of the black plans he and Selene had for her, an overwhelming rage came over me and shattered my usual self-control.

"Yes," said Bethany, her dark eyes on me. As with Alyce, I got the impression that she wasn't missing much. "I'd be interested in meeting her."

"In my opinion," I went on, "Morgan desperately needs to learn as much as she can as fast as she can. It's nerve-racking being around her, feeling like she could blink and make a building collapse."

"She's as powerful as that?" Bethany looked very interested.

"I think so. This is someone who has had barely any instruction, who's uninitiated and who has never even thought about going through the Great Trial. Someone who grew up having no idea of her powers, her heritage."

"Yet she shows such great promise?"

"She lights fires with her mind," I said, shrugging helplessly. "No one taught her how to do that. She has an inherent knowledge of power chants and other quite complicated spells that would be very difficult for a well-educated witch to do. She scries with fire. And a few weeks ago, she shape-shifted."

"Holy Mother," Bethany breathed. "What did she shift into?"

"A wolf."

For a few minutes Bethany Malone and I sat looking at each other, drinking our wine. "Goddess," Bethany said finally.

"Yeah," I said wryly. "It gets rather tense sometimes."

"I see," she said. "Tell me a bit about how you conduct your circles."

I went over our usual rites, our check-ins and meditation and energy-raising. Bethany listened attentively as I briefed her on the lessons I had led so far, about basic correspondences, purifying the circle, focusing skills. "Kithic has had some ups and downs," I concluded. "But in general the members are coming together in an interesting way, and I'm committed to helping them as long as they want to continue and as long as I'm in the States. It would be easy for them to get off track if they missed several circles."

"Yes," Bethany agreed. She set down her empty glass. "I'm intrigued, Hunter. I want to meet Morgan. I'm curious to meet these kids. I'd be happy to take over your circles while you're gone."

Relief flooded my body. Instinctively I felt that Bethany would bring good energy to the group, and the fact that she was recommended by Alyce set my mind at ease. "Brilliant," I said. "Thanks very much. The circles meet every Saturday night at seven, but the location changes. This Saturday it'll be at Jenna Ruiz's house—I'll give you directions."

I left half an hour later, a huge weight off my shoulders. Bethany was both strong and sensible; Kithic, and especially Morgan, would be safe in her hands.

"What time is it there?" I asked. I had called Sky when I got home but guessed I hadn't calculated the time difference correctly. Sky sounded sleepy and uncharitable.

"It's . . ." I pictured her craning around for a clock. "It's oh-dark-thirty," she finally said irritably. "What's up?"

Sky and I had grown up together; though I had two siblings and she had four, we were the same age and had compatible temperaments. Though neither of us was much given to sappy emotional outbursts, we were as close as brother and sister, and we both knew it. Now I told her my news as briefly as possible, picturing her almond-shaped black eyes widening under her golden eyebrows.

"Oh, Giomanach," she breathed, lapsing into my coven name, the name she had called me through childhood. "Oh, Goddess, I don't believe it—after all this time."

"Yeah. I leave on Saturday. It's about an eleven-hour drive, I think."

"I just can't believe it," Sky repeated. She paused. "How about I catch a flight back and go with you?"

I smiled with gratitude. "Thanks, Sky, but I'm all right going solo. Besides, you've done enough—I'd have never found them without you. You're on holiday."

I paused, and changed the subject. "How's the mighty Cara?" Sky's sister Cara was living in Paris.

Sky gave an uncharacteristic giggle. "She's pretty much the same: beautiful, successful, extremely popular, blokes panting at the door, constant promotions at work, the usual."

"Gross," I said. "And of course she's still sweet and kind and impossible to hate?"

Sky sighed. "Yes, damn her. She's been great. I'm glad I'm here. I still feel so—drained. Tired. Achy. I keep expecting to get the flu, but it hasn't come yet."

I waited, wondering if she would ask for news of Raven, but she didn't. "Listen," I said, "I'll call you from there and let you know what's happening. Who knows what I'll find? Anyway—I'll keep in touch."

"Do," she said. "I might be back in England, or maybe even America, by the time you get home. I don't know how much more fabulousness I can stand."

"Paris or Cara?"

"Both."

We rang off, and I sat for a moment, hoping that being away was doing her good. I frowned, thinking about how she was still feeling run-down. Was it just a simple mental thing, caused by stress or unhappiness, or was she really sick?

I knew Morgan's number by heart and braced myself to talk to one of her parents if they answered the phone. But it was Morgan who said, "Hello, Hunter."

Morgan's slightly husky voice sent shivers down my spine, and I realized I was gripping the phone a little tighter. You are pathetic, Niall, I told myself. "Hi," I said. "How are you?"

"Okay. Have you been getting ready for your trip?"

"Yes. I've lined up a replacement circle leader. Her name is Bethany Malone. Alyce recommended her, and I went to see her tonight. She seems terrific—I hope you'll like her. I think she'll be really good."

"Hmmm. I guess I just like it best when you lead the circles."

Morgan wasn't being coy or trying to inflate my ego. She was naturally shy, and it took her a while to be comfortable with new people. Making magick with people is an intimate thing: it's very hard to hold on to your barriers and defenses when you're connected by the energy. And Morgan wrote the book on defenses and barriers.

"I know," I said. "But Bethany is very learned, and it's a good opportunity for you to work with someone new. You know I'm not the best teacher for you." Because I want to ravish you.

She remained quiet, and I sensed that she was feeling conflicted about things.

"Hunter—I know you have to go," she said finally. "It's incredible that your folks are alive. You have to go see them. I know that. It's just—I'll miss you while you're gone."

"Love," I said. "I'm going to miss you, too. I wish I knew when I'll be back. I mean, I might be back in three days, or it might take a week . . . or longer."

"Uh-huh," she said, sounding down.

"I'll be thinking of you the whole time," I said. "I'll try to call as often as I can. And I'll be so glad when I'm back." Part of me felt almost guilty saying that. The truth was, I really had no idea what would happen. What if my parents no longer had to live in hiding? What if they could live openly and we could be a real family? Maybe they were planning to move back to England, to be near Beck and Shelagh. We would have actual family holiday celebrations, like for Ostara, coming up. Maybe next year's Yule would be truly joyous, with all of us together at last.

And if they did return to England, where would that leave me? I can easily work in England—plenty of witches are there. And I knew the council would be eager to send me out on another job soon. Nothing was holding me in Widow's Vale except Morgan. What if I had to choose between being with my parents or being with Morgan? If I could be near my parents, see them, make magick with them, learn from them . . . that would carry a lot of weight. And Morgan wouldn't be able to join me in England, not for at least a year and a half.

A lot can happen in a year and a half. A lot can happen in three months.

"I'll be glad when you get back, too," Morgan said. I sensed her taking charge of herself, deliberately deciding to be stronger. "But I know it'll be wonderful for you to go." Her voice sounded much more brisk and matter-of-fact.

"Thanks," I said softly, feeling the warmth of my love for her.

"I can't believe I can't go with you," she said. "But anyway—I was thinking, if you're leaving early Saturday, maybe we could have dinner together tomorrow night, just the two of us. Unless you think you're going to be really busy getting ready."

Terrific idea. "No, I'll make sure to get everything done before then. Dinner alone tomorrow sounds wonderful.

Let's do it at my house—I'll try to put something special together."

"Great," she said, and I picked up on her waves of relief and anticipation.

"I'll look forward to seeing you, love," I said.

"Me too," she said, and we rang off.

3.
Goodbye

I can't believe Hunter is leaving tomorrow. I feel a sense of dread when I think about him being gone. I tried to scry last night but really didn't pick up on anything except images of woods. Frustrating.

Now, on to the main thing. I've read in Maeve's Book of Shadows that blood witches can do spells to either get pregnant or not get pregnant. I went yesterday to Practical Magick and tried to find a spell, but I couldn't and was too embarrassed to ask Alyce. So this afternoon after school, I drove over to Norton, to the Planned Parenthood office there, and got a three-month supply of the Pill and a prescription to fill if I need to.

I parked down the street (so original) and crept up the block to the building, which of course had humongous letters on the side screaming Planned Parenthood! Catholic teenagers having premarital sex against their parents' wishes, step right up! Goddess, by the time I got inside the building, I was shaking with mortification.

If only I were Bree! Bree has her own gynecologist and suavely went on the Pill when she was fifteen. The whole thing only underlines how immature I am. Yet I do absolutely feel ready to go to bed with Hunter. I mean, I'm dying to. I've been wanting to, but things just haven't worked out. But tonight is going to be the night— I feel it.

I came home and took the first pill as instructed. We'll need to use a condom, too, because the pill doesn't kick in for a month and even though I trust Hunter, I'd rather be safe than sorry.

I can't believe I thought about doing this with Cal. I still feel incredibly sad when I think about him—sad that he's dead, that Selene destroyed his life, that I had anything to do with it. But I'm so glad I'm not with him and didn't go to bed with him. What I feel for Hunter is so different than what I felt for Cal. I love Hunter truly and deeply; I trust and admire and respect him. I feel sure that he loves me, that he will take care of me and not hurt me, and that he respects me as a person and doesn't just want to remake me into what he thinks would be a perfect girlfriend. I feel comfortable with him; I feel safe. I trust him.

And physically, oh, Goddess, he makes me crazy. So tonight's the night. Tonight I'm going to quit being a kid, a little girl. By tomorrow morning, I'll be a woman.
—Morgan

By Friday evening I was tightly wound. Everything was weighing on my mind: Should I stop the mail or ask a neighbor to gather it? Would my car make it to Canada? Did I have enough money? Thoughts consumed me as I surveyed the table I had set. I looked at it suspiciously, certain I'd forgotten something. Something for the trip, something for dinner? I couldn't think. Shaking my head, I tugged at the tablecloth and leaned over to light the candles. Dinner was basically done and waiting in the kitchen. I like to cook. I frowned: had I ever seen Morgan be picky about food? I couldn't remember—my brain was fried. In general, she has an appalling diet. For example, she considers Diet Coke to be an appropriate breakfast food. And she eats these thin, horrible pastries with a teaspoon of jam in the middle and frosting on top. Pop-Tarts. Goddess, it makes me ill just to think about it.

The doorbell rang, and I jumped about a foot in the air— I hadn't felt her coming up the walk. Automatically I pushed my hand through my hair, then remembered too late that always makes it stand up in a stupid way. Goddess, help me.

I opened the door, my heart already thudding. It was dark out, of course, and Morgan stood framed in our weak porch light, her brown eyes huge.

"Hi," I said, feeling awash in love for her. "Come on in."

She came in wordlessly and took off her coat. Hmmm— she was wearing some long skirtlike thing that swept the top of her clogs. Usually she wears jeans, so she had made a special effort for tonight, and I felt oddly pleased in an old-fashioned, male-chauvinist-pig kind of way. Her clingy brown sweater showed off her broad shoulders and her arms, which I knew were strong and toned. Once again the knowledge that she never wears a bra popped into my fevered brain, and I felt my knees start to go wonky. Her skin, and the curve of her waist, and the way she responded when I—

"Hunter?" she said, watching my face.

"Ah, yes," I said, snapping my mind back to reality. "Right. Hi, love." I put my hand on her back and leaned down to kiss her. She kissed me back, her lips gentle on mine, and I was struck by how alive she felt, how vibrant.

"Are you hungry?" I asked when we pulled apart.

She smiled, her eyes lighting up, and I laughed. "What am I saying? You're always hungry."

Half an hour later I was pleased by the fact that Morgan wasn't picky about food. While I wasn't sure if she knew the difference between bad food (instant tarts and diet soda) and good food (the linguine I had made for dinner), still, the fact that she ate everything and seemed to enjoy it was heartening.

"How did you learn to cook?" she asked, taking another thin slice of bruschetta.

"Self-defense. My aunt Shelagh was pretty uninspired. I couldn't blame her—she had years of cooking for twelve people at every meal before she caught on and started making the oldest kids help out."

Morgan laughed, and I felt the same kind of inner glow that came over me when I had worked a particularly nice bit of magick. I loved her. I didn't want to leave her. I wanted her to be packed, to be ready to get in my car tomorrow morning and drive off with me. Like her, I was frustrated by the fact that she was only seventeen.

"I brought dessert," she said, going into the parlor. She returned with a white pastry box and opened it at the table.

"Voilà. Two éclairs."

"Brilliant," I said, reaching for one. Witches and sweets seem to go together. I know that after spell-working, I tend to fall upon whatever sweet carbohydrate there is. Even Aunt Shelagh, during her macrobiotic period, had been observed wolfing down a brownie after a Lammastide rite.

As I fixed a pot of tea, I began to realize that Morgan was coiled almost as tightly as I was. I knew she was upset about me leaving tomorrow. I was both upset and incredibly excited. Part of me was aching to go jump in the car right now and set off, every minute bringing me closer to my long-lost parents. I tried as unobtrusively as possible to feel her aura. Regular people can't feel someone do this; even a lot of witches would be pretty unaware of it. I'd had a lot of training in feeling auras as a Seeker. It was literally my job to know people, to be able to detect nuances about their behavior, their energy.

"What are you doing?" Morgan asked.

I sighed. Served me right for trying to scan someone as strong as she was.

"Feeling your aura," I said, turning on the hot water in the sink. "You seem kind of . . . tense. Are you okay?"

She nodded, not looking at me, and drank the last of her tea. "Um, could you leave that till later?" she asked, gesturing toward the kitchen mess. "I just—want to be with you now. It's our last night, and I want us to spend time together, just us."

"Sure, of course," I said, turning off the water. I put my arm around her shoulders and led her from the kitchen.

She leaned against me. "Let's go up to your room."

All my senses jumped to full alert. "All right," I said, feeling my throat contract. Our chances to be alone and physical were few and far between, and I had been hoping we could take advantage of the opportunity tonight.

We walked upstairs, where Sky had one bedroom and I have the other. As we walked in, I could see all at once how impersonal the room seemed. Even after being in Widow's Vale for months, I hadn't spent much time settling in. The room contained my bed, my almost bare desk, and three boxes of books, which remained unpacked. There were no curtains, no rugs, no photographs or knickknacks. It was almost like walking into an abandoned dormitory. I felt a sudden embarrassment at the complete lack of mood.

Morgan left me and walked to the bed, which was still, after months of my living here, just a box spring and a mattress on the floor. She kicked off her clogs, sat down, and leaned back against the pillows. Then she looked at me and smiled. I smiled back.

My nerves jolted awake as desire flared to life. For once we didn't have to worry about Sky coming home; it was a weekend night, so Morgan wouldn't have to leave by nine; we had the rest of the evening together and an empty house with no disruptions. Then we were lying next to each other and I was kicking off my boots and my hands were reaching around her sides. The idea that Morgan was lying on my bed went right to my head, and then all thoughts fled as we kissed deeply, our mouths joined. Goddess, she felt good. I have always found her intensely attractive, everything about her: her body, her face, her scent, how she moved against me, the sounds she made as we kissed. I leaned into her, deepening our kiss.

"Hunter, Hunter," she said, pulling her mouth away from mine.

"Mmm." I followed her mouth, but her hands pressed against my chest and pushed. I swam toward coherence and looked into her eyes to see her gazing at me seriously. "What, love, too much?" Please don't say it was too much. "What?" I asked again.

"Hunter, I want us to make love," she whispered, her eyes glancing at my mouth. "I love you. I'm ready."

My brain struggled to process the words. Had I really heard that, or was this some cruel fantasy? I looked down at her face, her incredible, sculptured face. Was she serious?

I swallowed hard. "You want to . . ."

"I'm ready, Hunter," she said, her voice soft but sounding confident. "I want to make love with you."

It was as if the entire universe had just dropped literally into my lap. We had come close several times, and I had been keen to since practically the first moment I saw her, but it had never quite worked out.

"Are you sure?" I felt compelled to ask. *Please, please, please.*

She nodded, and my heart began to pound. "I started taking the Pill."

My eyebrows rose. She was serious; she had thought it out; she was ready. I sent out a huge, silent thank-you to the universe and pressed against her, holding her close.

"I really want that, too," I murmured against her hair. "I've been wanting to." I tried to quell the urgent impulse to simply leap on her—don't scare her off—and instead kissed her gently down the side of her face and neck. She wriggled to give me better access and made little sounds in her throat.

"Do you know about conception spells?" I asked, stroking her hair away from her face.

"Yes—but I couldn't find any, and I couldn't ask Alyce."

"When did you start taking the Pill?"

"This afternoon. I brought condoms, too."

I grinned at her, and after a moment she grinned back. "Right. We better do a barrier spell just to be safe," I said, and she nodded, her cheeks flushing a beautiful rose color. Pathetically, it had been a long time since I had needed one, and I had to look it up. In the interests of continuing her education, I explained the basics to Morgan and saw her eyes widen as she grasped the basic image. "Let me go do this, and I'll be right back," I said, running the tip of my tongue along the curve of her ear.

"Hurry," she said, looking extremely witchy, and I almost raced out of the room and stumbled down the hall to Sky's.

When I came back a few minutes later, Morgan was under the covers up to her shoulders. I took in the sight of her skirt, jumper, camisole, and her socks on the floor. *Oh, yeah,* I thought, yanking my shirt over my head and unsnapping my jeans.

"Come here, come here," she said, smiling and holding out her hands. Then I was sliding under the covers, feeling her skin against mine. At last, at last, at last. I held her head in my hands and kissed her deeply, again and again until we were both breathing fast and Morgan's eyes were glittering, her pupils wide and dark.

This was something I had been dreaming about for months. Her arms were clasped around my back, holding me close, pressing herself against my chest. Our legs were tangled together, hers long and smooth.

"I love you so much," I whispered, stroking her, caressing her, watching her eyes unfocus as she moved under my hands. I knew she hadn't done this before, and I wanted to make sure this was fabulous for her, that she was comfortable and happy.

"I love you, too," she said, her voice sounding tight. She moved against me restlessly, twining closer to me as if she had been doing this all her life. Her hands moved over my skin, over my chest, around my back, stroking my face. . . .

"Oh my God," she breathed.

"Yes," I said, lost, leaning in to kiss her neck.

"Hunter," she whispered back. "Yes."

"This is so right," I muttered, kissing her. "You're everything to me."

She made an indistinguishable reply. I never dreamed my last night here would end so perfectly, I thought dimly. Tonight we were going to make love.

I couldn't believe this was actually happening, that Morgan had decided she was ready. What timing—this would be the perfect memory to have when I was far away in . . . uh, far away in . . . Canada.

I will miss this so much when I am . . . in Canada. Far away in Canada. Tomorrow. Uh . . . I quickly tried to push away those bothersome thoughts. Focus, I ordered myself. Concentrate. You have Morgan in your bed.

"I'll think about this the whole time you're gone," said my love's voice, and I felt her breath against my cheek.

The whole time you're *gone*. "Mmm," I breathed as I felt

her tongue tickling my ear. Goddess, this was fun, this was perfect; I was here with Morgan, *Morgan,* who I loved and wanted so much. So much for having an early night—I wanted to do this all night long until the sun came up and—

Oh, bloody hell. When the sun came up, I would be taking off. I didn't know how long I would be gone. I didn't know what I was going to find. I could find something that would change my life forever. My parents had been on the run from Amyranth for eleven years. I could be heading into serious danger. Or I could be heading into having a family for the first time in eleven years. A family I wouldn't want to leave.

And then where would I be? Away from Morgan. And who would I be? Someone who slept with his girlfriend right before leaving her.

Damnation.

"Hunter?" She sounded worried, and I looked down and touched her face.

"It's nothing," I told myself as much as her. I closed my eyes and kissed her again, feeling how right it was, how incredible. What was I doing? Should I be doing this? Was this a good idea?

It was a fantastic idea, and I pulled her against me more tightly, feeling sweat break out on my forehead. Morgan had thought about this, had decided she was ready, and Goddess knew I was. We were going to do this tonight. How could I possibly stop now?

I couldn't; there was just no way. Tonight was all about Morgan and me. Morgan, who trusted me. Trusted me not to hurt her. Oh, no. No. I pulled my weight back onto my arm. Morgan's eyes were wide. "Did I—is something wrong?"

The insecurity in her voice made me jerk my head down to look at her. "No!" I said strongly, holding her closer. "No, of course not."

"Then what's going on?" She snuggled closer to me, and once again I had to fight a vicious battle between the top half of my body and the lower half. The top half, which included my barely functioning brain, won, but only by a minuscule margin.

I sighed. "Morgan—I'm wondering . . . is this the best idea?" The words caught in my throat, but I forced them out, feeling like I should be awarded a *big* medal for valor and chivalry.

"Whaaat?" she said, drawing back from me. I felt her aura, her vibrations instantly change. They had been incredibly strong, vibrant, involved, excited. Now they were cooling, stilling rapidly as she retreated. No, no, no, I wanted to howl.

Talk fast, Niall. "Morgan," I said, still trying to hold her close. "Listen—I want to make love with you practically more than I want to breathe at this very moment. But is this really the best thing? I mean, I'm leaving tomorrow; I don't know when I'll be back; I don't know what I'll find or what will happen to me while I'm there. I'm saying my future is somewhat up in the air at the moment. It seems—irresponsible for me to make love with you now."

"Irresponsible?"

I winced at the cool tone in her voice, and she pulled away from me physically and emotionally while I swore to myself in four different languages, including Middle Gaelic, which isn't easy.

"Love, this is killing me," I said with complete sincerity. "I want this very much. And here you are, giving yourself to me, and it's our first time, and it's incredible. I absolutely don't want to hurt you. But—what if something happens that keeps us apart? I don't want to do this just once and then forget about it. I want our first time to be only the first in a long, long series of us being together."

"I don't understand."

"Wait—stop." She had scooted to the side of the bed, and the sight of her bare, beautiful back, stiff with anger and hurt, pained me almost as much as the athame she had once sent into my neck a long time ago. "Please, Morgan, wait. Hear me out." I lunged and grabbed her around the hips, my cheek pressed against her back as she tried unsuccessfully to get up. "I'm dying to sleep with you!" I said. "I'm mad with wanting you! There's nothing more that I want than to be in bed, making love, all night long!"

"Except to be responsible."

"Morgan! Just think for a minute. Do you really think that the night before I leave for Goddess knows how long is the best time for us to sleep together for the first time? I mean, if we had been sleeping together for a while, this would be fine. But this is our first time together. It should be perfect. It shouldn't be part of a good-bye."

Her jaw barely moved. "In your opinion." Icicles dripping. She took advantage of my momentary appalled shock to leap out of bed. I scrambled after her, wondering where the hell I had thrown my underwear. In seconds she had pulled on her camisole with the lace and was reaching for her sweater and socks.

"Morgan, Morgan," I said, looking desperately around the floor. "This isn't my decision alone. We need to agree on this. I mean, I *hate* this. All I want to do is make love with you. But can you try to see where I'm coming from, a little bit?"

The look she gave me was distant, and my heart dropped down to my bare knees. She shrugged and sat on the bed to pull on her socks. "I don't get it. You want to, but you won't. You love me, but you won't sleep with me. I feel like a leper."

I ditched all thoughts of underwear and pulled on my jeans, being careful with the zipper. "Morgan, I want you more than I've ever wanted anyone in my whole life. And I'm ecstatic that you feel ready for us to go to bed. That's what I've wanted ever since I met you." I knelt down in front of her and looked up into her eyes, her shuttered face. "I love you. I'm so attracted to you. Please believe me. I mean, you *felt* it. This has nothing, *nothing* to do with how much I want you or how sexy you are. It's just about timing."

"Timing." She sighed and lifted her long hair away from her neck, then let it fall. I thought of it spread over my sheets, over my pillows, and began to think I was completely mad.

"Morgan, I don't want to hurt you. But either option is bad: if I ask you to wait for the next time we can be together, it hurts your feelings and makes you think I don't want you. Which isn't true. But if we go to bed tonight and then something happens and we're apart for a long time, would that be better?"

She glanced away, seeming for the first time to examine the state of my room. Great. I saw her gaze trace the bare floor, the gutted candles on my desk, the boxes still unpacked.

With no warning, an image of Cal Blaire's bedroom came to mind. I had seen it when I'd been in Selene's house, undoing spells, setting other spells. Cal's bedroom had been huge, quirky, and romantic. His bed had been an antique, hung with mosquito netting. Everything in that room had been beautiful, luxurious, interesting, seductive. Feeling bleak, I rested my face on my outstretched arm, wondering if I had just buggered things up in a really huge way.

"Morgan, please," I said. When I raised my head, she was examining me calmly, and I damned her ability to rein in her strongest emotions. I covered her hand with one of mine, and she didn't flinch. "Please don't be angry with me or hurt. Please don't leave like this. Please let's have tonight be a good thing for both of us. I don't want this to be the moment we both look back on while I'm gone."

My words seemed to reach her, and I felt the sharp edges of her anger soften. A tiny bit. Then her face crumpled, and she said, "Hunter, you're leaving tomorrow. I want us to be joined together in a real way before you go. Here I am, I'm seventeen"—she threw out her arm in a disgusted, disbelieving gesture—"and you're *nine*teen and can be with anyone you want, and I want you to feel connected to me!" Her voice broke and she clenched her fists, looking embarrassed and angry with herself for seeming weak.

Her words completely threw me, and I gaped at her. One of my favorite Tynan Flannery quotes came back to me: "Women are impossible, witches are worse, and women who are powerful witches are going to be the death of me."

I reached up and enfolded her in my arms, resting my head against her chest just under her chin. "Love, we *are* joined together in a real way because I love you, and you love me. We're mùirn beatha dàns," I said quietly. "You say I can be with anyone I want—well, you can be with anyone you want, too. I choose to be with you. Who do you choose?" I tilted my head back and looked up at her.

"I choose you," she muttered ungraciously, and I wanted to laugh but had enough sense left not to.

"I feel connected to you," I went on. "And it doesn't have anything to do with us having sex. Not that I don't want to have sex!" I added hastily. "I definitely want to have sex! Make no mistake! The second I come back, I'm going to jump you, wherever you are, and initiate you into the sublime joys of womanhood."

She burst into laughter, and I grinned. "My mother will be thrilled," she said dryly.

"Me too," I promised with intense sincerity, and she laughed again.

We sat there, hugging, for a long time. I hoped that we had somewhat mended our earlier rift, and I again started to question whether or not I should just go for it. Hell, Morgan wanted to, I wanted to, it would make us happy . . . for the next couple of hours. What about after that? I was conducting a debate within myself when Morgan gently disengaged from me.

"It's late. I better go."

"Uh . . ."

She kissed me, holding my face in her strong hands. "Drive carefully tomorrow. Call me when you can. I'll be thinking about you."

Then she stood up and left, her clogs loud on the stairs. I

trotted after her, still trying to figure out what I wanted. She turned and gave me a last, wistful smile, and then she was gone. I sat down on the steps, unsure of what had happened between us, unsure if I had done the right thing, unsure about everything.

4.
The Journey

February 1992

Today the world seems like a different place than it did yesterday. I've always loved the winters here, but now the sky seems cold and pitiless. The beauty of our world seems to have dimmed a little. Yesterday Mama and I were calm and safe, secure in our lives and most especially in our magick. But last night Mama got a witch message from Aunt Celine. A seeker had come to "investigate" her library, and he found some dark spells she had written—a weather spell and a spell for bending another's will, spells Mama says she never even used. But according to the council—the idiot council, Mama calls them—just writing these spells shows a leaning toward dark magick that can't be tolerated. And Aunt Celine committed what Mama calls the cardinal sin: she argued with the Seeker, tried to make it seem like the spells aren't all that dangerous. Mama says the Seeker couldn't accept another point of view; he thought it was dangerous. And Aunt Céline was stripped of her powers today.

Oh, Goddess, it is such a horrible ceremony, but Mama insisted that we scry to watch it all. She says that I am old enough to see such things, that I have a duty to make myself aware of the abuses of power that are committed in our world. Aunt Céline cried and shook, and when she was finally stripped, she looked like a broken bird: no longer able to fly, only half the person that she was before. Mama says that the council is corrupt and stupid, that they don't understand the value of knowledge. I don't know what to believe. I only know that what happened to Céline was terrifying. I can't imagine anything she could have done to deserve such a terrible fate.

— J. C.

After Morgan left, I felt sad and wished I could have the whole evening to live over again. When would I ever learn?

I awoke at six in the morning, in the dark and inhospitable dawn. The house seemed empty and too quiet and once again I missed Sky's presence. I hoped she was feeling better in France.

A hot shower revived me, and I finished loading the car, seeing my breath come out in dragon puffs. I decided to have breakfast on the road and set off for the highway. Just before leaving Widow's Vale, I pulled over and performed one last spell, sending it out into the world, knowing it would come to fruition about twenty-four hours from now.

Then I headed north, toward Canada and my parents.

"A room!" I bellowed into the barely functional intercom. "Do you have a room!"

I rubbed my bleary eyes and waited for the crackly response, hoping they spoke English. For the last sixty miles every sign had been in French. I don't speak French—not well, anyway. I was forty minutes away from Quebec City, had been driving for hours, and was starting to nod with tiredness, though it wasn't much past seven. I needed food, another hot shower, and a bed.

My parents' town, Saint Jérôme du Lac was only about four hours away, and the temptation to press on was strong. But that would involve crafting wake-up spells for myself or drinking a hell of a lot of coffee, and it meant I would get to my parents' house after ten o'clock at night. A worrying thing—I had been unable to reach them by phone or scrying or witch message. I doubted they knew I was coming. If I was going to show up unannounced after eleven years, it should probably be in the daytime.

The intercom crackled back at me, and I took the garbled response to be an affirmative. Twenty minutes later I was tucking into some *jambon* and *oeufs,* washing them down with *bière,* in the tiny restaurant next door. Half an hour after that, I was facedown on the bedspread in my small, cinder block room, dead out. I didn't wake up till nine the next morning.

On Sunday the first thought I had, after "Where the hell am I?" was about Morgan. I pictured her slowly coming to recognize the spell I'd crafted before I left. I pictured her eyes widening, a smile softening her mouth. It had been hardly more than a day, but I missed her, ached for her, and felt lonely without her.

But today was the day. I was within four hours of seeing my parents, and the thought shook me to my very bones. This was the day I had been waiting for for more than eleven years. My heart sped up in anticipation.

I leaped up, showered, and hit the road by ten. I'd bought a road map of Quebec Province back in New York. Now it led me up Highway 40, around Quebec City, then off to a smaller, two-lane highway, number 175, that would take me north to Lac St. Jean, a big lake. Saint Jérôme du Lac was about forty minutes from there, from what I could tell.

This far north, any signs of approaching spring were wiped out. Trees were still bare and skeletal, patches of crusted snow lay everywhere in shade; no crocuses or snowdrops bloomed anywhere. Spring's warm tendrils had not yet touched this country and wouldn't for some weeks, it appeared.

Following my map carefully, I turned off onto Highway 169, still heading north. I knew I had to go about 120 kilometers to reach St. Jérôme du Lac and, with any luck, could do it in about an hour. Now that I was so close to my parents' home, a strange, quivery feeling was beginning in my stomach. My hands felt sweaty on the steering wheel; my pulse quickened; my gaze darted around the scenery surrounding me, attuned to any movement. I was nervous. I hadn't seen my parents in eleven years. What would they be like?

Eleven years ago, I had barely come up to my da's breast-bone. Now I was probably as tall as he. The last image I had of my father was that he was big, stern, and invincible. He hadn't been scared of anything. Sometimes I had seen a deep sadness in his eyes, and when I had asked about it, he'd replied that he'd been thinking about the past. I didn't under-stand it then but now knew that he'd probably been thinking about his life before he married Fiona, my mum. He'd been married before, to Selene Belltower, a fact that still stunned me. He'd had another son, a few months older than I, whom he'd abandoned. That had been Cal Blaire. Now both Cal and Selene were dead, and people were glad of it. I won-dered if Da knew. Probably not.

My mum was Da's perfect counterpart: soft, smiling, femi-nine, with a ready laugh, a sense of mischief that delighted us kids, and an easy, immediate ability to show emotion. It was Mum who explained Da's moods, Mum who comforted us, cheered us on, encouraged us, loved us openly. I had been des-perate to please both of them, for different reasons. Childishly, as I drove closer to them with every mile, I felt a barrage of dif-ferent emotions—loss, anger that they had been gone, a quick-ening sense of anticipation. Would I, when I saw them, be once again able to lean on my da, to rely on his strength? Would I feel that he would protect me still, though I was now grown and come into my full powers? Hell, I was a Seeker for the council—the youngest ever. Yet I was still a nineteen-year-old

kid, and the thought that I could abandon the weight of being a
Seeker, even if just for a short while, was very seductive.

They would have changed in the past eleven years, I
knew. Of course I knew it. I had changed, too. But we were
still family, blood family, still father and mother and son.
Somehow we would make those relationships fit us once
more. And soon I would contact Alwyn, too, and the four of
us could be a true family again.

The small turnoff road to Saint Jérôme du Lac was clearly
marked. Suddenly I was bumping down a road that hadn't
been re-tarmacked in what looked like twenty years. Huge
potholes caught me off guard, and I bottomed out twice
before I wised up, dropped down to about twenty miles an
hour, and drove like an old lady.

The farther off the main road I got, the less prosperous
the land felt. I went through several tiny, poor-looking towns,
each with a petrol station that might or might not function. I
also saw a lot of Canadian Indians, who called themselves First
Nations people, and signs for First Nations crafts and displays

I had no idea how far down this road I was supposed to
go; after that first sign, I hadn't seen any more indications that
I was heading in the right direction. Finally, when it seemed
that I had gone impossibly far, I gave up and pulled over to get
petrol. After I had filled the tank, I went into the small store
attached to the station to pay. The storekeeper had his back
to me; he was on a small wooden ladder, stocking packages
of sandpaper. I hoped he spoke English.

"Excuse me," I said, and when he turned around, I saw
that he must be part Indian.

"Yes?"

"I put in ten dollars of regular petrol," I said, laying the Canadian money on the counter.

"Okay." The cash register was beautiful: an old, manually operated one.

A sudden thought struck me, and in desperation I said, "Do you by any chance know of any English or Irish people who live around here?"

He thought for a moment. "You mean the witch?" he said, and I gaped at him.

"Uh . . ."

"The only English I know around here is the witch," he said helpfully. "He moved here two, three months ago."

"Um, all right." My mind was spinning. It was unheard of to be known so casually in a community. Even witches who weren't hiding from Amyranth were always very circumspect, very private. We never would have identified ourselves as witches to anyone. Why did this man know? What did that mean? And why did he only mention a "he"?

"Could you tell me where they live?" I asked, with a sense of dread. Surely if this man knew about them, knew where they lived, then Amyranth did, too. What would I find when I got there?

"Sure. Let me draw you a map."

I watched in a daze as the man quickly sketched a rough map. I thanked him and headed back to my car. I didn't know what to think, so I started the engine and set off. The crude but accurate map led me down back roads that were even more bumpy and ill kept than the access road had been. I wished I had rented an SUV and hated the thought of what my car's undercarriage must look like.

I was hungry, thirsty, and exhausted. I began to wonder if this whole trip had been an unworkable spell. Then I came upon a little wooden shack, the first building I'd seen in ten minutes, set back from the road. A battered Ford Escort minus its wheels stood on cinder blocks in the yard. Dead ivy vines clung to it. The yard was a wintry mess—untidy, overgrown, littered with trash. It didn't look like anyone lived here. Obviously this wasn't my parents' house, though it seemed to be in the correct place on the map. I must have gotten it wrong. No witch would live in a house in this condition, with this kind of general air of neglect and poverty. A glance around the back confirmed my suspicions: Even in Canada, in winter, I should have been able to detect a cleared plot for an herb garden. But there was nothing, no sign of one. I sighed and rubbed my cold hands together.

Finally I decided to at least knock and try to get directions. I climbed up onto the porch, pulling my coat around me. This close, I felt I could detect the presence of a person, though it wasn't strong or clear, which was unusual. I knocked on the rough, unpainted door, wincing as my cold bare knuckles rasped the wood.

Inside, there was a slight shuffling, then silence, and I knocked again. Come on, I thought. I just want directions. With no warning I felt something touch my presence, as if someone had cast their senses to identify me. My eyes widened in surprise, and then the door slowly creaked open, admitting dim light into the dark interior. My eyes instantly adjusted, and I saw that I was standing before Daniel Niall, my father, for the first time in eleven years.

5.
Grief

This morning I woke up, and yes, Hunter was still gone. My heart went thunk, and I thought of the days stretching before me without him, no Hunter to talk to or see or hold. Dagda and I were pondering this bleak reality when Mom tapped on my door and asked if I was going to church with them. Spontaneously I said yes, knowing that services would take up two hours of Hunterless time and maybe distract me for a while. So I showered and dressed and went downstairs and got sent back upstairs by my parents because I looked like a schlub. I borrowed a dress from Mary K. that fortunately is too long for her.

It started when we stepped outside. At first I thought I was imagining things—it didn't make sense. But then I thought, Oh, Goddess, and realized that Hunter must have crafted a spell before he left town yesterday.

It was beautiful magick. I had no idea how he had done it, but I knew that he had, and I almost started crying. It was almost everywhere I looked, all morning: in the shapes of tree branches, in the plume of smoke from Dad's car's exhaust, in the curve of Mom's scarf as it lay over her shoulder. Somehow Hunter had woven letters and symbols and runes into almost everything I saw: crossed branches made an H̲, for Hunter. A crooked line of leaves in the street made an M̲, for Morgan. I saw the rune Ken, for fire and passion, and blushed, remembering Friday night. My heart lightened when I saw Geofu: One of its uses is for strengthening relationships. And in the line of pale gray clouds floating above us I saw Peorth: hidden things revealed and also female sexuality. Oh, Goddess, I love him so much.

—Morgan

I've read books where people are "struck speechless," and to me it always sounded like they just couldn't think on their feet. The ability to think on my feet has always been one of my strengths, but it deserted me now as I gazed at the man before me.

I knew what my father looked like: Though I had brought no photographs with me to America, I had my memories, and they had always seemed accurate and consistent and full. But they didn't match this person in the doorway. This couldn't be Da. It was an incredibly bad Da imitation, a hollowed-out husk of what once had been my father. My gaze darted restlessly over him, taking in the sparse gray hair, the hollow cheeks with their deep lines, the thin, almost emaciated body. His clothes were shabby, his face unshaven, and there was a dank smell of stale air emanating from the dark house.

My father is only forty-six. This person looked about sixty.

He frowned at me consideringly but without wonder: He didn't recognize me. I had a sudden, irrational urge to turn and run—something in me didn't want to know how he had come to be in this state. I was afraid. Then, slowly, as I stood there, a dim light entered his eyes; he looked at me more closely; he measured me up and down, trying to calculate how much his son would have grown in eleven years.

A vague disbelief replaced the suspicion in his eyes, and then we were hugging wordlessly, enfolded in each other's lanky arms like tall spiders. In my memories, my father was tall, huge. In real life I had an inch or two on him and outweighed him by maybe two stone. And I'm not hefty.

My father pulled back and held me at arm's length, his hands on my shoulders. His eyes seemed to memorize me, to memorize my pattern, my imprint. Then he said, "Oh, Giomanach. My son." His voice sounded like a thin, sharp piece of slate.

"Yes," I said, looking behind him for Mum. Goddess, if Da looked like this, what would *she* look like? Again I was afraid. In all my thoughts and wishes and dreams and hopes and expectations about this meeting, it had never occurred to me that I would be hurt emotionally. Physically, yes, depending on what happened with Amyranth. But not emotionally. Not feeling pain because of who my parents had become.

"You're here alone?" Da rasped, and looked around me to examine the yard.

"Yes," I said, feeling incapable of intelligent speech.

"Come in, then."

I stepped through the doorway into the darkness. It was daylight outside, but every window was shuttered or curtained.

The air was stale and unpleasant. I saw dusty herbs hanging from nails on the wall, a cloth that looked like an altar cloth, and candles everywhere, their wax spilling over, their wicks guttered and untrimmed. Those were the only signs I could see that a witch lived in this house.

It was filthy. Old newspapers littered the floor, which was black with dirt. Dust was thick on everything. The furniture was old, shabby, all castoffs, put out on the junk heap and rescued—but not fixed up. The one table I saw was covered with piles of paper, dried and crumbling plants, some Canadian coins, and unsteady stacks of plates with bits of crusts and dried food.

This house was shocking. It would have been shocking to find anyone living in it, but to find a witch living in it was almost unfathomable. Though witches are notorious pack rats—mostly related to their ongoing studies of the craft— just about all of us instinctively create order and cleanliness around us. It's easier to make magick in an ordered, purified environment. I looked around to find Da shuffling his feet awkwardly, glancing down as if embarrassed for me to be seeing this.

"Da, where's Mum?" I asked outright as tendrils of fear began to coil around my heart. My father staggered as if hit and bumped against the doorway leading into what I guessed was the kitchen. I reached out to steady him, but he pulled away and ran his bony hand through his unkempt hair. He looked at me thoughtfully.

"Sit down, son," came his thin, stony voice. "I've imagined this conversation a thousand times. More. Fancy a cuppa?"

Through the doorway I saw that the kitchen was, if anything, even more filthy than the lounge. Unwashed pots and crockery covered every surface; the tiny cooker was black with burned grease; packages of opened food bore unmistakable signs of having been shared by mice. I felt ill.

"I'll make it," I said, and started rolling up my sleeves.

Twenty minutes later Da and I were seated in the room's two armchairs; mine wobbled, and the vinyl seat was held together with silver duct tape. The tea was hot, and that was all I could say for it. I'd run the water in the sink till the rusty hue had gone and scrubbed the kettle and two mugs. That was the best I could do.

I wanted to cry, "What the hell is going on? What's happened?" but instead sipped my tea and tried not to grimace. I hadn't known what to expect—I'd had images, thoughts, but no solid way of knowing what my reunion with my parents would be like. However, this scene, this reality, hadn't come close to being on the board.

"Where's Mum, Da?" I repeated, since no answer seemed forthcoming. Something deep inside me was afraid I already knew the answer, but there was no way I couldn't ask it.

Da visibly flinched again, as if I had struck him. The hand holding his tea mug trembled almost uncontrollably, and tea splashed over the rim onto the chair's arm and onto his raggedy brown corduroys.

"Your mum's dead, son," he said, not looking at me.

I gazed at him unwaveringly as my brain painfully processed the words one by one. They made no sense to me, yet they also made a horrible kind of sense. My mother, Fiona, was dead. In our coven some people had called her Fiona the Bright because being around her, with her flaming red hair, was like raising your face to a ray of sun. Da had called her Fiona the Beautiful. Us kids, when we were little and childishly angry, sometimes called her Fiona the Mean. And giving no respectful weight to our words, our anger, she would laugh at us: Fiona the Bright. Da was telling me she was dead, that her body was dead and gone. I had no mother and so no future chance of experiencing a mother's love, ever again in my life.

I couldn't cry in that house, that horrible, dark, lifeless house, in front of this person who was not the father I had known. Instead I rose, put down my tea, and staggered out the door to my car. I climbed in, coatless, and stayed out there until I was half frozen and my tears were under control. It was a long time, and Da didn't come after me.

When I went back in, Da was in exactly the same place I had left him, his cold, undrunk tea by his hand. I sat down again and shoved my hair off my forehead and said, "How? Why?"

He looked at me with sympathy, knowing all too well what I was feeling. "Fiona had battled ill health for years—since right after we left. Year after year we went from place to place, searching for safety. Sometimes she would do a little better, mostly she did worse. In Mexico, seven years ago, we had another close call with the dark wave—you know what that is?"

I nodded. As a Seeker, I had all too much experience with the dark wave.

"And after that it was pretty much downhill." He paused, and I stayed silent. "Your mother was so beautiful, Giomanach," he said softly. "She was beautiful, but more than that, she was good, truly good, in a way few witches are. She was light itself, goodness itself. Do you remember what she looked like?" His eyes on me, suddenly sharp.

I nodded again, not trusting myself to speak.

"She didn't look like that anymore," he said abruptly. "It was impossible for her not to be beautiful, but every year that passed took its toll on her. Her hair was white, white as a cloud, when she died. She was thin, too thin, and her skin was like . . . like paper, like fine paper: just as thin, just as white, as brittle." He shrugged, his shoulders pointed beneath his threadbare flannel shirt. "I thought she would die when we found out about Linden."

My head jerked up. "You know?"

Da nodded slowly, as if acknowledging it created fresh waves of pain that he could hardly bear. "We knew. I thought that would kill her. But it didn't—not quite. Anyway. This past winter was hard. I knew the end was coming, and so did she. She was tired, so tired, Giomanach. She didn't want to try anymore." His voice broke, and I winced. "Right before Yule she gave up. Gave me one last beautiful smile and slipped away, away from the pain, the fear." His head dropped nearly to his chest; he was trying to not cry in front of me.

I was upset, angry, devastated—not just at the news of my mother's death, but at the haggard condition of this man who appeared to be my father. Tense with inaction, I jumped up and began throwing open curtains, opening shutters. Pale, watery wintry sunlight seemed to consider streaming in, then decide against it as too much trouble. What light did enter only illuminated the pitiable condition of the house. I could see now why Da kept it dark.

This wreck of a man, this shell with his caved-in chest, his head bowed in pain and defeat, this was my da! This was the man whose anger I had feared! Whose love I had craved, whose approval I had worked for. He seemed pathetic, heartbreaking. I could only imagine what he had been going through, and going through alone, all this time. Had my mother's death done this to him? Had Amyranth? Had years of running done it? I sank back into my chair in frustration. Two months my mother had been dead. Two months. She had died just before Yule, a Yule I had celebrated back in Widow's Vale, with Kithic. If I had come here before Yule, I would have seen my mother alive.

"What about since then?" I asked. "What have you been doing since then?"

He looked up, seeming bewildered at my words. "Since then?" He looked around the room as if the answer was contained there. "Since then?"

Oh, this was bad. Why had he agreed to talk to the council? What was the point in all this? Maybe Da knew what bad shape he was in. Maybe he was hoping for help. He was my father. And he had the answers to a thousand questions I'd had since I was eight years old.

I tried again. "Da, what made you and Mum leave in the first place? How could you—how could you leave us behind?" My voice cracked and splintered—this was the question that had tormented me for more than half my life. How many times had I cried it aloud? How many times had I shouted it, screamed it, whispered it? Now here was the one person who could answer it, or so I hoped. Mum no longer could.

Da's eyes, once deep brown, now looked like dim pools

of brackish water. They focused on me with surprising sharpness, as if he had just realized I was there.

When he didn't answer, I went on, the questions spilling out like an unchecked river—once started, impossible to stop. "Why didn't you contact me before Mum died? How did you know Linden died? How could you not have contacted us when each of us was initiated?"

With each question my father's head sank lower and lower. He made no reply, and I realized with frustration that I would get no answers, at least not today. My stomach rumbled with alarming fierceness, and I remembered I had eaten nothing since that morning. It was now five o'clock, and dark.

"Come on, Da, let's get something to eat. We could both use it." Without waiting for a reply, I went into the kitchen and began opening cupboards. I found a tin of tomatoes, a tin of sardines, and some half-eaten, stale crackers. The refrigerator offered no joy, either: nothing but a lone turnip, whose shriveled, lonely form increased my confusion, my concern. Why was there no food in the house? What had he been eating? Who the hell eats *turnips?* I went back out to the living room, seeing again how thin Da was, how fragile he seemed. Well, I was here, and I was the only son he had left, and I would take care of him.

"On second thought, let's go out. I saw a diner in town. Come on, my treat."

6.
Turloch-eigh

June 1997

Today my cottage seems filled by a cloud of sadness. I know that this isn't a day for sorrow; it should be a day for happy memories, for quiet contemplation and reminiscing. Yet the sorrow comes along unbidden. Today is the fifth anniversary of Mama's death.

It seems so long ago that we lived in this house together, yet I remember so much about her—her intensity, her passion for learning, the way she strove to kindle in me an appreciation for the complexity of the world. And her morality. If they knew the truth of her beliefs, many witches who revere her today would not consider my mother a moral person. Yet her heart was large, her empathy complete. She taught me healing spells and did her utmost to help animals, children, anyone who was vulnerable. She had a strong sense of right and wrong, and she felt that our family had been wronged too many times. I miss her so terribly, even five years after her death. I would like to believe that somewhere, wherever her soul is on its journey, she is aware of the work I am doing, and she is proud.

Today I stayed away from the library. I did not want to be tempted; it would be so easy to hurt my mother in my nostalgia and my sadness. But tomorrow I will return to my work. I will continue compiling . . . continue learning.

I cannot think of a better gift that I could give to Mama.

—J. C.

"Sorcier."

My head jerked at the French word, so casually spoken, as a man walked past Da and me. We were in the town proper of Saint Jérôme du Lac, which was basically one street, no stoplight. One petrol station. But at least there were sidewalks and some small shops that had a quaint, frontiersy charm. I had parked my car not far from the town's only diner, which was right next to the town's only grocer. It was dark and colder than an ice cave. I pulled my coat tighter around my neck and wondered that my father didn't get knocked over

by the stiff breeze. And then I'd heard it: *"Sorcier."* Witch. I
know the word *witch* in at least seventeen different languages:
useful for a Seeker. *Bruja* in Spanish. *Hexe* in German. Italians
call us *strega*. Polish people say *wiedźma*. In Dutch, I listen for
toverheks. Once in Russia I had old potatoes thrown at me
while kids yelled, *"Koldunya!"* Long story. In Hungary one says
boszorkány. And in French Canada one says, *"Sorcier."*

But why anyone from the town would identify my father
as a witch was still a mystery. I resolved to ask him about it
later, after we ate. Two more people greeted Da as we went
into the diner. He acknowledged them with a bob of his
head, an embarrassed nod. I scanned them with my senses:
they were just townspeople.

I, for one, felt better after a dinner of sausage, potatoes,
canned green beans, and four thick slices of a rough brown
bread that was incredible. I felt self-conscious, sitting with
Da; I felt eyes on me, speculation. Da introduced me to no
one, never said my name aloud, and I wondered if he was
being careful or if he had forgotten who I was.

"Eat that," I encouraged him, gesturing at his plate with
my fork. "I paid good money for it."

He gave me a slight, wan smile, and I found myself hun-
grily looking for a trace of his old, broad grin. I didn't see it.

"Your mother would be amazed to see my appetite so
small," he said, forcing a laugh that sounded more like a cough.
"She used to tease me about being able to eat for three."

"I remember," I said.

Da picked his way through his meal and left so much on his
plate that I was forced to finish it for him. He did seem a little
less shaky afterward, though. I bet he would be a hundred

percent better after I got a couple more good meals into him.

Luckily the grocer's was still open after dinner. I bought a cabbage, some potatoes, some apples. Da, not even pretending to take an interest, sank down into a rocking chair near the door, his head on his chest, while I shopped. I bought meat—missing the somewhat intimidating sterile American packaging—chicken, fresh fish, and staples: flour, rice, sugar, coffee, tea. Inspired, I bought laundry detergent, other cleaning supplies. I paid for everything, collected my dim ghost of a father, and loaded groceries and Da into the car.

By the time we got back down the road to the cabin, Da was a waxy shade of gray. Worriedly I helped him into the dark house, felt unsuccessfully for a light switch, gave up, and used witch sight to lead him to a tiny, bleak, horrid bedroom—the only one in the house. It was about the size of a walk-in freezer and had about as much charm. The walls were unpainted pine planks spotted with black, age-old sap. The rusty iron bed, like the furniture in the living room, looked like it had been saved from a garbage heap. Unwashed clothes were piled in small heaps on the floor. Next to the bed was a small, rickety table, covered with candles, dust, and old cups of tea. Da sank down onto dingy sheets and rested his arm across his eyes.

"Da—are you ill?" I asked, suddenly wondering if he had cancer or a death spell on him or something else. "Can I get you something? Tea?"

"No, lad," came his reedy voice. "Just tired. Leave me be; I'll be fine in the morning."

I doubted that but awkwardly pulled a thin coverlet over him and went out into the lounge. I still couldn't find a light switch but brought in the groceries, lit some candles, and looked around. The cabin was freezing. As cold as outside. Shivering, I searched for a thermostat. Ten minutes later I came to the sinking realization that there was no thermostat because the cabin had no electricity.

Smothering a curse, I lit more candles. How had Da managed to live like this for any length of time? No wonder he looked so bad. I'd thought all the candles and lanterns had been witch gear—but they were his only light sources as well.

There was a fireplace with some handfuls of pale ashes scattered on its hearth. Of course there was no firewood inside—that would be too easy! I pulled on my coat and tramped around in the snow outside. I found some firewood, wet with snow. Inside I kindled a fire, and the flames leapt upward, the damp wood sizzling. Instantly the room seemed cheerier, more inviting. The fireplace was small but threw back an impressive heat into the frigid room.

Da was sleeping, and I was bone tired but filled with a frenetic energy that wouldn't admit to fear. I had been on the road since morning; it had been a long, strange, awful, sad day. I was in a cabin in the backwoods of Canada with my unrecognizable, broken father. I heard wolves in the distance, thought of Morgan, and missed her with such a powerful ache that I felt my throat close. I wanted to sit down in one of the vinyl recliners and weep again but knew that if I started, I wouldn't stop. So instead I rolled up my sleeves and went into the kitchen.

At midnight I sank down onto a couch I hadn't even realized was there because it had been covered with litter. I pulled an ancient, ugly crocheted afghan over me and closed my eyes, trying to ignore the hot tears that burned my cheeks.

*   *   *

In the morning I was awakened by the sounds of my father shuffling out of his room. He walked through the lounge without noticing me on the couch, then stopped in the kitchen doorway. I waited for his response. Last night, after thanking the Goddess for the propane-run refrigerator, stove, and hot water heater, I had done a major clean of the kitchen. Da stood there, and then he seemed to remember that if the kitchen looked like this, someone else must be in the cabin, and he looked for me. I sat up, swinging my long legs over the side of the couch.

"Morning, Da," I said, standing and stretching.

He managed a smile. "I'd almost forgotten you were here. It's been too long since someone said good morning to me," he said wistfully. He gestured at the kitchen. "You do all this?"

"Aye."

"Ta. I just haven't been up to much lately—I know I let the place get into a mess." Then he went into the kitchen and sat down at the table, and suddenly I remembered how he used to do that in the morning, just come in and sit down, and Mum would make him a cup of tea. Grateful for any reminder of the old days, I filled the kettle with water and set it on the stove. I fixed him tea and toast with butter, which he managed to eat a little bit of. For myself I fried eggs and some rashers of bacon: fuel for the day's labor ahead. I sat down across from Da and tucked in. I still had a thousand questions; he was still the only man who could answer them. I would have to choose my time.

After breakfast I set him to work, helping me clean the rest of the house. While I was piling papers and things neatly on the desk so I could wipe the surface, I couldn't help noticing letters from people, crude notes written in broken languages, hand-written thank-you notes in English and French, praising my da, praising his skill as a *sorcier*. With shock I realized that Daniel Niall, Woodbane, formerly of Turloch-eigh, son of Brónagh Niall, high priestess of Turloch-eigh, was basically the local medicine man, the village witch. I couldn't believe it. Surely this was incredibly dangerous. As far as I knew, Da hadn't worked real magick for years because it would be one way for Amyranth to trace him. Was it now safe? Why, and how?

Burning with questions, I went to find Da and sighed when I found him asleep again, on the bare mattress in his room. It had only been about an hour since I'd started him on the candles and lanterns. Well, sleep was probably good for him. Sleep and food and someone looking out for him.

In the meantime, I couldn't just sit around this place. I felt a need to get out, breathe fresh air. In the end I made Da a sandwich and left it covered on the kitchen table. Then I bundled up every piece of cloth in the place, threw it into the boot of my car, and headed for the laundromat in town.

"What do you do with your trash?" I asked Da at dinner. There was quite a mound of black plastic trash bags in the front yard. Sadly, they actually didn't make the yard look that much worse.

He looked up from his boiled potato. "Take it to the dump, outside town."

I groaned silently. Great. Now I'd have to haul it all in my car. After we ate for a few more minutes, I said, "Da, all I know is what Uncle Beck told me, what I've heard whispers of from other people through the years. But now I'm here, across from you, and you've got the answers. I need to know: Why did you and Mum leave us? Why did you disappear? And why is it now all right for me to know where you are?"

He didn't look at me. His bony fingers plucked restlessly at the cuff of the clean flannel shirt I had given him to put on. "It's ancient history, lad," he said in a voice like a dry leaf. "It was probably all a mistake. Won't bring your mother back, anyway." A spasm of pain crossed his face.

"I know it won't bring Mum back," I said. I took a swig of beer, watching him across the table as though he might disappear in a puff of smoke to avoid my questions. "That doesn't mean I shouldn't know the answers. Look, Da, I've waited eleven years. You took my life apart when you left, and Linden's, and Alwyn's. Now I need to know. Why did you and Mum leave?"

Though I'm only nineteen, I'm a Seeker. Which means I make my living by asking people questions. I've grown used to waiting for answers, asking over and over until I find out what I want to know. I'm very good at my job, so I said again, very gently, "Why did you and Mum leave? It's almost unheard of for a coven to split up if trouble's coming."

Da shifted in his seat. He held his fork and patted a piece of cabbage on his plate, pushing it this way and that. I waited. I can be very patient.

"I don't want to talk about it," he said at last. His eyes flicked up at mine, and I noticed again how their color had faded, had clouded. But there was a hint of sharpness in his gaze, and in an instant I knew that my father still had some kind of power and that I needed to remember that. "But you always were like a bulldog—once you got your teeth in something, you didn't let it go. You were like that as a lad."

I met his eyes squarely. "I'm like that still, Da," I said. "Actually, I've made a career of it. I'm a Seeker for the council. I investigate people for a living."

I watched Da's eyes, waiting for his reaction. Would he be proud of me? I had always imagined he would be, but then, so many of my imaginings had been proven hopelessly wrong in the last twenty-four hours. My father looked at me considering, and then his face broke into a sudden smile.

"So you are," he said softly. "Well, that's quite an accomplishment, son. Right, then, bulldog, if you'll have it out of me—Selene sent the dark wave after us, at Turloch-eigh."

I frowned, my brain kicking into gear.

"Us who?" I asked.

He cleared his throat. "Your mother and me . Both of us. Your mother felt it that night, felt it coming, knew who it was aimed at. Knew who it was from."

"Was Selene finally getting you back for leaving her? The dark wave that killed the entire village was about Selene's jealousy?"

He gave a short bark of a laugh. "Yes. She'd always said that I would need to look over my shoulder the rest of my life. And she was right. Well, until now." He paused. "At least *they* were able to come together again safely."

"How's that?" I wasn't sure if I had heard him correctly. "Who came together again?"

Da was looking at me, frowning. "Gìomanach, what have you been thinking all these years? That we were gone, along with everyone else, and we never came back for you and you didn't know why?" He shook his head. "Oh, Goddess, forgive me. And I ask your forgiveness, too, son." He swallowed, then went on.

"No. That night Fiona felt the dark wave coming. We knew it was for us, and us alone, but that Selene and Amyranth would be happy to destroy the whole village if it included us. So, taking a chance, the only chance we could, we fled, leaving you three there, spelled with protection circles. We thought if we left, we would draw the dark wave away from the village. That it would follow us, instead of concerning itself with Turloch-eigh. Later, when I scried and saw the village gone, I was devastated—our flight hadn't saved anything. But years later Brian Entwhistle found me. You remember Brian, right?"

I searched my memory and came up with a big, ruddy bear of a man. I nodded.

"It wasn't safe to contact you kids or Beck. Too risky. But once or twice we were contacted by older witches, powerful ones who could protect themselves. Brian was one. I was astonished when he found us—thought he'd been dead all those years."

I was sitting on the edge of my seat, my hands gripping the arms. Here it was, the whole story, after so long. It wasn't what I'd thought it would be.

"Brian told us that you kids were safe, that Beck had gotten you. He told me the village had actually been spared."

"But wait a minute," I said, remembering something. "I went back there, not three years ago. The place is deserted and has been for years. No one lives there. I saw it."

"Yes, they all returned a short time after the dark wave left—trickled back in one family at a time. They tried to make another go at it there, but apparently the dark wave came too close. It left a destructive spell in its wake. After everyone had come home and settled down, things started happening. Accidents, unexplained illnesses. Crops failed, gardens died, spells went wrong. It took a year of that before the whole village up and moved closer to the coast. They made a new town there, thirty miles away, and Brian told me they had prospered."

I was dumbfounded. "So everyone left and no one bothered to look for us? They left me and Linden and Alwyn to die?"

"They didn't know you were there, lad. Susan Forest knocked on our door that night. Mum and I had already fled. You kids slept like the dead and were spelled besides. Fiona and I wanted you to sleep soundly, not to wake up in the middle of the night and find us missing and be afraid." Da's voice caught there, and he shook his head as if to clear it. "Anyway, when she got no answer, she figured we'd all taken off."

I shook my head, frowning in disbelief. "All this time I've been mourning not only my parents, but everyone I knew, everyone in our village. And now you're telling me they're hale and hearty, living thirty miles from home. I don't believe this!" I said. "Why didn't anyone contact us at Beck's? Why hasn't anyone told me this before?"

Da shrugged. "I don't know. I guess Beck probably knows. Maybe he thought that if you knew, you'd leave him and go back to the village."

"Why didn't Brian Entwhistle bother to tell us that our parents were alive?" I was feeling a growing sense of indignation. All those years of tears, of pain . . . so much of it could have been avoided. It made me ill to think about it.

Da met my eyes. "What would you have done if you'd known?"

"Come to find you!" I said.

"Right."

Oh.

"Your mum and I thought that if we sacrificed ourselves, we could save our children, save our coven. When I scried and saw the village gone, it was a hard blow. I thought it had been for nothing. I was relieved when I found out my vision had been wrong."

"But after you learned that the coven was safe, why didn't you come back?"

"The dark wave was still after us. I'm not sure if it was always Selene, but at the time we reckoned it was. No one's ever hated me like that. Goddess willing, no one ever will. At the time, it seemed that if we kept Selene occupied with finding us, she'd have less time to go after other covens, other witches. It seemed worth it." He shrugged, as if that were no longer so clear.

"Why aren't you in hiding now?" I asked. "Are you not in danger anymore?"

My father let out a deep breath, and again I was struck by how old he seemed, how frail. He looked like my grandfather. "You know why. Selene's dead. So's Cal."

I nodded. So he *did* know. I figured the council must have told him when they'd found him with Sky's lead. I drank my tea, trying to digest this story. It was light-years away from anything I had imagined.

"So now you work magick, now that you're not hiding from Amyranth?"

Da shrugged, his thin shoulders rising like a coat hanger in his shirt. "Like I said, Fiona's dead," he said. "No point in hiding, in keeping safe. The one thing I wanted to protect is gone. What's the point in fighting anymore? It was for her I kept moving, kept finding new sanctuaries. She wanted us to stick to this plan; I wanted to do what she wanted. But she's gone now. There's nothing left to protect." He spoke like an automaton, his words expressionless, his eyes focused on the table in front of him.

By the time he finished talking, my face was burning. On the one hand, I was glad that he and Mum had had some noble cause behind their disappearance, glad they had acted unselfishly, glad they had been trying to protect others. But it was also incredibly hurtful to listen to my own father basically negate my existence, my dead brother's, my sister's. Obviously staying alive now for our sakes hadn't occurred to him. I was glad he had been loyal to my mother; I was angry that he had not been loyal to his children.

Abruptly I got up and went into the living room. I undid the huge bundle of washing in the lounge, then made up Da's bed with clean sheets and blankets. He was in the same position when I got back to the kitchen.

"I'm so sorry, son," he said in a thin voice. "We thought we were acting for the best. Maybe we helped some—I hope we did. It's hard to see clearly now what would have been best."

"Yes. I see that. Well, it's late," I said, not looking at him. It was only eight-thirty. "Maybe we should turn in."

"Aye. I'm knackered," Da said. He got up and shuffled with his old man's walk toward the one bedroom. I sat down at the kitchen table, had another cup of tea, and listened to the deep silence of the house. Again I missed Morgan fiercely. If she were here, I would feel so much better, so much stronger. I imagined her arms coming around me, her long hair falling over my shoulder like a heavy, maple-colored curtain. I imagined us locked together, kissing, rolling around on my bed. I remembered her wanting to make love with me and me saying no. What an idiot I'd been. I resolved to call her the next day as soon as I could get into town.

I washed up the few dishes and cleaned the kitchen. By ten o'clock I felt physically exhausted enough to try to sleep. I wrapped myself up in a scratchy wool blanket and the ugly afghan. After being washed, the afghan was only about half as big as it had been. Oops.

From the couch I extinguished the lanterns and candles with my mind, and after they were snuffed, I lay in the darkness that is never really darkness, not for a witch. I thought about my unrecognizable da. When I was younger, he'd seemed like a bear of a man, huge, powerful, an inevitable force to be reckoned with. Once when I was about six, I had been playing near an icy river that ran by our house. Of course I fell in, got carried downstream, and only barely managed to grab a low-hanging branch. I clung to it with all my strength while I frantically sent Da a witch message. It was long minutes before he came leaping down the bank toward me and splashed into the strong current. With one hand he grabbed my arm and hauled me out, flinging me toward the bank like a dead cat. I was shaking with cold, blue and numb, and mainly he felt I'd gotten what I'd deserved for being so stupid as to play near the river.

"Thanks, Da," I gasped, my teeth chattering so hard, I almost bit my lip. He nodded at me abruptly, then gestured to my wet clothes. "Don't let your mum see you like that." I watched him stride up the bank and out of sight, like a giant, then I crawled to my knees and made my way home.

But he could be so patient, teaching us spells. He'd begun on me when I was four, simple little spells to keep me from burning my mouth on my tea, to help me relax and concentrate, to track our dogs, Judy and Floss. It's true I caught on quickly; I was a good student. But it's also true that Da was an incredibly good teacher, organized in his thoughts, able to impart information, able to give pertinent examples. He was kind when I messed up, and while he made it clear he expected a lot from me, still, he also made me feel that I was special, smart, quick, and satisfying to teach. I used to swell like a sponge when he praised me, almost bursting in the glow of his approval.

I turned on my side, trying to find a position that coordinated the old couch's lumps with my rib cage. I heard Da sleeping restlessly in the other room, as if he didn't even know how to do a soothing spell. Like yourself, idiot, said my critical inner voice. I rubbed the bridge of my nose with two fingers, trying to dispel a tension headache, then quickly sketched a few runes and sigils in the air, muttering words I'd know since childhood. *Where I am is safe and calm, I am hidden from the storm, I can close my eyes and breathe, now my worries will all leave.* What second-year student doesn't know that? I said it, and instantly my eyes felt heavier, my breathing slowed, and I felt less stressed.

Just before I fell asleep, I remembered one last scene with my father. I had been seven and full of myself, leagues ahead of the other third-year students in our coven. To show off, I had crafted a spell to put on our cat, Mrs. Wilkie. It was to make her think a canary was dipping about her head so she would rear up on her hind paws and swat at it over and over again. Of course, nothing was there, and we kids were hysterical with laughter, watching her pointlessly swipe at the air.

Da hadn't found it so funny. He came down on us like the wrath of heaven, and of course my companions instantly gave me up, their fingers pointing at me silently. He hauled me up by my collar, undid the spell on poor Mrs. Wilkie, and then marched me to the woodshed (a real woodshed) and tanned my bum. I ate standing up for three days. Americans seem to be much more skittish about spanking, but I know that after that, I never again put a spell on an animal for fun. His approval was like the sun, his disapproval like a storm. I got love and affection from Mum, but it was being in Da's good stead that mattered.

Today his approval or disapproval would mean little to me. With that last sad thought, I fell asleep.

7.
Le Sorcier

December 2001

Today I found a bit of rock that had a thread of gold running through it. I held it in my hand and closed my eyes and felt its ancient fire warming my hand. I came home, crunching through the snow, and set the rock on my kitchen table. I stoked the fire and made myself some mulled cider. Then we sat together, the rock and I, and it told me its secrets. I knew its true name, the name of the rock and the name of the gold within it. Using the form as described by Davina Heartson, I gently, slowly, patiently coaxed the gold out of the rock. It came to me, running like water on fire, and now it sits in a tiny lump in my hand, the rock being empty where it was. It was such a beautiful

thing, such a pure power, such a perfect knowledge, that I sat there and wept with it.

This is the value of my research. This is why
I've gone to such lengths to collect true names.
Knowing true names elevates my magick into something different from what most witches have. I
was born strong—I'm a Courceau. But the collec-
tion of true names I have gives me almost
unlimited power over the known ones. Think of
what I could do with some particular names.
Think of what power I would wield. I could be
virtually unstoppable. Then I could avenge my
family, all those who have had their power
stripped, who have been persecuted, misunderstood,
judged by small-minded bureaucrats. They didn't
understand who they were dealing with. I will
make it my life's work to teach them.

—J. C.

When I got up the next morning, Da was gone, just like
he had been the day before. I wondered if the extra food
he'd been getting had given him more energy, because he'd
said he was going to "work." Work? What work? I tried
engage him in a conversation about it but got nowhere. I
could only assume that this had something to do with the
notes thanking him for his skill as a *sorcier;* perhaps he was
out on medicine-man business. I wished he would tell me
more about it, because he scarcely seemed strong enough to
go to the grocery store, never mind tending to the magickal

needs of villagers. The previous afternoon when he had come home, his face had been the color of a cloudy sky. I wondered if his heart was okay. When was the last time he had seen a healer? I wished I could get him to one. As far as I knew, though, he was the only witch around.

But he was gone again, already gone when I woke up.

I meditated, fixed myself breakfast, then drove to town to call Morgan. Naturally, I discovered that if you phone your seventeen-year-old girlfriend at ten o'clock on a Tuesday, she'll be in school. After that disappointing episode, I hung around the house. I was starting to feel like a professional maid. I scrubbed the lounge floor (it was wood—who'd've known?), whapped all the dust out of the furniture, and did a complete overhaul of the kitchen cabinets. I didn't know how long I'd be there or what Da would do after I was gone, but I'd laid in a good store of supplies.

Back in New York, I had pictured quite a different family reunion. I'd pictured my parents—changed, to be sure, but still themselves—overjoyed to see me, my mum crying tears of joy, Da clapping me on the back (I've grown so tall!). I'd pictured us sitting round a table, the three of us, sharing good stories and bad, sharing meals, catching each other up on our lives of the last eleven years.

I hadn't pictured a gray ghost of a father, my mother being dead, and me being Suzy Homekeeper while my da went off to his secretive work that the whole bloody village knew about but I didn't. I'd wondered if my folks would be impressed or unhappy about my Seeker assignment from the council. I'd wondered if they'd test my magickal strength, if they would be happy with my progress, my power. I'd wanted to tell them about Morgan and even talk to them about what had happened with Linden, and with Selene and Cal. But Da had showed no interest in my life, asked no questions. Two of his four children were dead, and he hadn't asked any more about it. He hadn't asked about Beck or Shelagh or Sky or anyone else.

Goddess, why had I even come? And why was I staying? I sighed and looked around the cabin. It gave me a sad satisfaction: everything was tidy and scrubbed, clean and purified, the way a witch's house should be. I had sprinkled salt, burned sage, and performed purifying rites. The cabin no longer jangled my nerves when I walked into it. I had dragged it into the light. It was too bad the ground outside was still frozen—I was itching to start digging up earth for a summer garden plot, every witch's mainstay. Sky and I had planned ours back in January. I hoped she would come back soon to help me with it.

Then my senses picked up on someone approaching the cabin—Da returning? No. I turned off the gas burner on the stove and cast my senses more strongly.

When I answered the knock, I found a short First Nation woman standing on the porch. I didn't think I'd seen her in town.

Her dark eyes squinted at me, and she didn't smile. *"Où est le sorcier?"*

I still found it hard to believe that my father was identified as such so openly. In danger or not, it's never considered a good thing to be so obvious, so well known. Witches had been persecuted for hundreds of years, and it always made sense to be prudent.

I searched my mind for the little French I'd learned to impress an ex-girlfriend. *"Il n'est pas ici,"* I said haltingly.

The woman looked at me, then reached out her hand and touched my arm. I felt her warmth through my sweater. She gave a brisk nod, as if a suspicion had been confirmed. *"Vous être aussi un sorcier,"* she said matter-of-factly. *"Suivez-moi."*

My jaw dropped open. Where was I? What was this crazy place where witches lived openly and villagers could tell them from nonwitches?

At my hesitation she said again, more firmly, *"Suivez-moi,"* and gestured toward a dark blue pickup truck that looked as though it had fallen down a rocky ravine, only to be hauled out and pressed into service again.

"Oh, no, ah . . . ," I began. I had no intention of getting into a truck with a strange woman, not in the backwoods of Canada, not when my da wasn't around.

"Oui, oui," she said with quiet insistence. *"Vous suivez-moi. Maintenant."*

"Uh, *pourquoi?*" I asked awkwardly, and her jaw set.

"Nous besoin de vous," she said shortly. We need you. *"Maintenant."* Now.

Oh, blimey, I muttered to myself. *"D'accord, d'accord,"* I said, turning inside. I banked the fire in the hearth, grabbed my coat, and, wondering what the hell I was getting myself into, followed the woman out into the rapidly falling darkness.

The inside of the truck felt as rough as the outside looked. Nor did this driver believe in seat belts. I clutched the door handle, feeling my kidneys being pummeled by every stone and hole in the road, and there were too many to count. After what felt like a whole evening but was really only about twenty minutes, we slowed and the truck's headlights illuminated a cabin much like my father's, and in the same state of decrepitude.

As soon as I unfolded myself painfully from the truck, I picked up on waves of searing pain and distress. My eyes widened, and I looked at the woman. What the hell was this about? Did she need a witch or a doctor? My driver came and took my arm in a deceptively strong grip and almost hauled me up the steps. I braced myself and started summoning strength, spells of power and protection, ward-evil spells.

Inside the cabin my ears were immediately assaulted by a long, howling wail of pain, as if an animal were trapped somehow. There were three other First Nation people in the lounge, and I saw another, older woman bent over the stove in the kitchen, which looked marginally better equipped than Da's. Four sets of black eyes fastened on me as I stood there, dumbfounded, and then I cringed as the unearthly wail came again.

The woman tugged off my coat and pulled me toward a bedroom. Inside the bedroom I was confronted by something I never could have predicted: a woman in childbirth, writhing on a bed, while an elderly woman tended to her. In a flash I realized I had been brought here as a healer, to help this woman give birth.

"Oh, no," I began lamely as the woman screamed again. It made all the hairs on the back of my neck stand up, and I was uncomfortably reminded of the time when Morgan had shape-shifted into a wolf.

"Vous elle aidez," said my driver in a no-nonsense tone.

"Oh, no," I said, trying to find my voice. "She should be in hospital." Did anyone here understand some English? I was rapidly running out of French. I glanced at the bed again and saw with dismay that in fact it wasn't a woman in childbirth— it was a teenager who couldn't have been more than sixteen or seventeen. Morgan's age. And she was having a hard time of it.

"*Non. Vous elle aidez,*" my companion said, a shade more loudly and with more tension.

"A hospital?" I said hopefully, and couldn't help shuddering when the girl screamed again. She didn't seem to know I was there. Her shoulder-length black hair was soaked with sweat, and she clutched her huge belly and curled up as if to get away from the pain. Tears had wet her face, so there was no dry skin left. The older woman was trying to soothe her, calm her, but the girl was hysterical and kept batting her away. The tension in the room was climbing rapidly, and I could feel coils of pressure surrounding the whole cabin. Oh, Goddess.

The older woman looked at me. "The 'opital is five *heures* far. Far." She gestured with her hand to mean "extremely far away." "Is big money, big money."

Bloody hell. The girl wailed again, and I felt like I was in a nightmare. A huge swooping attack from Amyranth right now, with Ciaran trying to rip my soul away, would almost have been more welcome. The older woman, who I guessed was a midwife, came toward me. The girl sobbed brokenly on the bed, and I felt her energy draining away.

"I get *bébé* out," the older woman said, using descriptive hand motions that made my face heat. "You *calmez* 'er. *Oui? Calmez.*" Again she gestured, with soothing, stroking motions, then pointed toward the girl.

There was nothing for it: I had to step into the fray. The

girl's eyes were wild, rolling like those of a frightened horse; she was fighting everyone who was trying to help her. My nerves were shot, but I reached deep inside my mind and quickly blocked things out, sinking into a midlevel meditative state. After a few seconds I began to send waves of calmness, comfort, reassurance to the girl. I didn't even try to interact with her present self but sent these thoughts deep within her, into her mind, where she would simply receive them without examining or questioning them.

The girl's wild, terrified eyes slowly turned and focused on me. Then another contraction racked her, and she coiled and screamed again. I had never done anything like this before and had to make up a plan as I went along. I kept sending waves of calm, comfort, reassurance toward her while I desperately searched my spell repertoire for anything that might help. *Right, come on, Niall, pull it out of your hat.* I stepped closer to the bed and saw where it was soaked from her water breaking. Agh. I wanted to run from the room. Instead I looked away and began to sketch sigils over the bed, muttering spells to take away pain, spells to calm fears, spells to make her relax, to let go, to release.

The girl made harsh panting sounds, *hah, hah, hah,* but kept her eyes on my face. As if in a dream, I slowly reached out and touched her wet hair, like black silken rope beneath my fingers. As soon as I touched her, I got a horrible wave of pain, as if someone had run a machete through my gut, and I gasped and swallowed hard. The girl wailed again, but already her cry was less intense, less frightened. She tried to slap my hand away, but I dodged her and stayed connected, pushing some of my own strength and energy into her, transferring some of my power. Within half a minute she had quit struggling, quit writhing as much. Her next contraction broke our connection, but I came back, touching her temple, closing my eyes to focus. The poor teenage girl couldn't begin to understand, but the deep-seated, primal woman within her could respond. Concentrating, I tuned that woman into the cycles of nature, of renewal, of birth. I sent knowledge that the contractions weren't the pain of injury or damage, but instead signs of her body's awesome power, the strength that was able to bring a child into the world. I felt the consciousness of the child within her, felt that it was strong and healthy, a girl. I smiled and looked up. My driver and the midwife were nearby. The midwife was sponging the girl's forehead and patting her hand. *"Une fille,"* I said, smiling. *"Le bébé est une fille. Elle est jolie."*

At this the girl met my eyes again, and I saw that she understood, that she was calm enough to hear and understand words. *"Une fille,"* I told her softly again. *"Elle est jolie."* I tried to think of the word for healthy but couldn't. *"Elle est bonne,"* was the best I could come up with. The midwife smiled, and so did the woman who had fetched me, and then I sensed another contraction coming.

This time I reached down and held the girl's hand, and as her muscles began their tremendous push down, their intense concentric pressure, I tried to project the feeling that these contractions were just her body working hard to accomplish something. This was what she needed to do to get her baby out; she had to release her fear and let her body take over. Her body, like the bodies of women since time began, knew what to do and could do it well. Together we rode the wave of her contraction, squeezing our hands together as it crested, and then I think we both panted as the force ebbed and her muscles relaxed again.

"*Oui, oui,*" murmured the midwife. She was down at the end of the bed, pushing the girl's knees up, and besides that I didn't want to know. I stayed near the head of the bed, looking into the girl's bottomless black eyes, holding her hand, sending calming waves. Her eyes were much calmer and more present; she looked more like a person.

"*Elle arrivé,*" the midwife murmured, and the girl's face contorted, and fast, fast, I sent images of things opening up, flowers blooming, seeds splitting, anything I could think of in my panicked state. I thought relaxation, concentration, releasing of fear, surrendering to her own body. As I looked at her, her eyes went very wide, her mouth opened, she said, "Ah, ah, ah, ah," in a high-pitched voice, and then suddenly it seemed like she kind of deflated. I made the mistake of glancing over to see the midwife pulling up a dark red, rubbery-looking baby, still connected to her mother by a pulsing blue cord. Sweat broke out on my forehead and my skin grew cold, as if I were about to faint. The baby squinched up its quarter-sized mouth, took a breath, and wailed, sounding like a tiny, infuriated puppy.

My patient's face softened, and she instinctively reached out her arms. The midwife, beaming now, wrapped the kicking, squalling baby in a clean towel and handed her to the mother, the cord stretching back behind her. As if the entire episode of terror and gut-splitting pain had never happened, the girl looked down at her baby and marveled at it. Feeling somewhat queasy, I looked at the infant, this end product of two people making love nine months earlier. Her face was red and raw looking. She had a cap of long, straight black hair that was glued to her little skull with what looked like petroleum jelly. Her skin was streaked with blood and white goop, and suddenly I felt like if I didn't have fresh air, I would die.

I staggered to my feet and lurched from the room, through the lounge and out the front door. Outside, I took in great, gulping breaths of icy air and instantly felt better. Somewhat embarrassed, I went back in to find that some of the other women had come into the bedroom. They were smiling, and I felt their waves of relief and happiness. They praised the girl, who was now beaming tiredly, holding her new daughter close. The midwife was still busy, and when I glanced over, she was picking up the cord, so I looked away fast.

I had never seen a human birth before and wished I hadn't seen this one. Yes, it was a miracle, yes, it was the Goddess incarnate, but still. I would have given a lot just then to be sitting in a pub, knocking back a pint and watching a football game on the telly.

The girl looked up and saw me, and she smiled widely, almost shyly at me. I was struck by how regular she looked, how girlish, how smooth her soft tan skin was, how white her teeth were. The contrast with how she'd been, while racked with pain and fear, was amazing. I smiled back, and she gestured to the baby in her arms.

"*Regardez elle,*" she murmured, smoothing the baby's

cheek. The baby turned her head toward her and opened her rosebud mouth, searching.

Quickly I said, *"Elle est très jolie, très belle. Vouz avez bonne chance."* Then I cornered the woman who had brought me and took her arm. "I have to go home now."

We were interrupted by other women thanking me gravely, treating me with distant gratitude, then turning, all warmth and smiles, to the girl. They knew I had helped the girl but also knew I was a witch and probably couldn't be trusted. I had mixed feelings. Surely a girl this young ought not to be having a baby. From looking around, I could see these people had no money; who knew how many of them lived in this four-room cabin? Yet seeing how the women clustered around the girl, praising her, admiring the baby, tending to them both, it was clear that the girl was safe here, that she would be treated well and her baby looked after. There was love here, and acceptance. And often, that was most of what one needed.

I tapped my driver's arm again—she was cooing over the baby, who was now attempting to nurse. I kept my eyes firmly away from what I considered a private thing (I was the only one who thought so—there were at least five other people in the room). "I have to go home now," I said again, and she looked up at me with impatience, and then understanding.

"Oui, oui. Vous avez fatigué."

Right. Whatever. I looked for my coat and shrugged it on. My right hand was sore from being squeezed so tightly. I suddenly felt bone weary, mentally and physically exhausted, and I was ashamedly aware that out of all of us, I had done the least work. Men might have bigger muscles, bigger hearts and lungs, but women have greater stamina, usually greater determination, and a certain patient, inexorable will of iron that gets hard things done. Which is why most covens are matriarchal, why lines in my religion usually went from mother to daughter. Women usually led the hardest, most complicated rites, the ones that took days, the ones that took a certain ruthlessness.

I sighed and realized I was punchy, my shoulder brushing against the door frame as I went through. The night air woke me up, making me blink and take in deep breaths. I groaned audibly as I saw my nemesis, the blue pickup truck from hell. The woman, whose name I had never learned, walked briskly to it and pulled herself into the driver's seat. I climbed into the passenger seat, pulled the door closed, and reflexively clutched the door handle.

Then the door of the cabin opened, and a sharp rectangle of light slanted across the dark yard. *"Attendez!"* cried a woman, and came toward us. She gestured to me to roll down my window, but it didn't unroll, so I opened my door. *"Merci, merci beaucoup, m'sieu sorcier,"* the woman said shyly. I saw that it was the older woman who had been in the kitchen.

I smiled and nodded, uncomfortable about being openly identified as such. *"De rien."*

"Non, non. Vous aidez ma petite-fille," she said, and pushed a package toward me.

Curious, I opened the brown paper and found a warm loaf of homemade bread and, beneath it, a somewhat new man's flannel shirt. I was incredibly touched. Right then I broke off a piece of the bread and bit it. It was incredible, and I closed my eyes, leaned back against the truck seat, and moaned. The women laughed. *"C'est très, très bon,"* I said with feeling. Then I unfolded the shirt and looked at it, as if to assess its quality. Finally I nodded and smiled: it was more than acceptable. The woman seemed relieved and even proud that I thought her gift was fine. *"Je vous remercier,"* I said formally, and she nodded, then clutched her shawl around her shoulders and ran back into the house.

Without another word, my chauffeur started the engine and hurtled us down an unpaved road that I couldn't even see, but she obviously knew by heart. By holding on to the door handle with one hand, I was still able to break off chunks of warm bread with the other and eat them. I was happy—I had done a good day's work—and then I remembered that I had been there only because Da hadn't.

"Daniel—*souvent il vous aidez?*" I said, butchering French grammar.

The woman's dark eyes seemed to become more guarded.

I motioned back to the cabin. *"Comme ça?"* Like that?

"Comme ça, et ne comme ça," she said unhelpfully.

"Do you speak any English at all?" I asked, frustrated.

She slanted a glance at me, and I thought I saw a glimmer of humor cross her face as I flinched, going over a pothole.

"Un peu."

"So Daniel helps you sometimes?" I asked in my neutral Seeker voice. As if the answer didn't matter. I looked out my window at the dark trees that flashed past, lit momentarily by the truck's unaligned headlights.

A slight frown wrinkled the skin between her brows. *"Quelquefois."* She hesitated, then seemed to make up her mind. "Not so much *maintenant*. Not so much. Good people, only when so desperate. Like today."

Every Seeker instinct in me came to life. "Good people?"

She looked away, then said in a voice I could barely hear over the engine, "People who don't walk in the light—they go to *le sorcier* more often."

Oh, Goddess, I muttered to myself. That didn't sound good. We were both silent the rest of the ride. She pulled up in front of Da's cabin but didn't shut off the engine.

"Merci," she said quietly, not smiling. *"Elle est ma fille, vous aidez."*

"Soyez le bienvenue." Then I got out of the truck, knowing that I would probably never see her, her daughter, or her new granddaughter again. Her tires spun on the snowy dirt behind me as I went up the steps to the porch. Inside, my father was there, in the kitchen, eating some meat I had browned hours ago. He looked up as if surprised to see me still around.

"We have to talk," I said.

8.
Answers

In the time I've been here, I've come to fully appreciate the pristine and harsh beauty of winter. Five years ago it was spring that made me feel alive, the unstoppable power and bursting rawness of life renewed. Now that seems so naive. For me, winter is the culmination of nature's beauty, winter that shows the perfection, the bare bones of the world I live in.

Today I walked for miles, up to Grandfather's Knee. The air was sharp and cold, like a knife, and by the time I reached the top, every breath seared my lungs. I felt alive, completely connected to everything around me. The sound of ice cracking in the sun, the rare, startled flight of a bird, the occasional wet drop of snow from a tree limb —all these things filled me, awoke my senses, until I felt almost painfully joyful, painfully ecstatic. I fell to my knees in the sun-softened snow and blessed the Goddess and the God. My entire life felt like a song, a song that was reaching a crescendo, right then.

Ahead of me lay a meadow, its snowy surface marked by animals who had come to break through the crust to forage. As I knelt there, I was startled by a flash of dusty white—a winter hare, zigzagging crazily across the meadow, running so incredibly fast that I could hardly follow it with my eyes. It was beautiful, a slightly darker white than the snow, designed to run, its feet sure and strong. A second later I saw the reason for its flight: a red-tailed hawk, its wingspan more than four feet, was swooping toward it. In the time it took me to blink, the hawk had swung its feet down and up and was already beating the air with its wings, heading skyward with its prize.

I didn't think. There was no time. Instinctively I traced a sigil and cried, "Israthtac! Israthtac!"

As if shot, the hawk faltered in midair, one shoulder dipping, its wings beating arrhythmically. I sent the message, "Drop it. Release." And in the next moment the hare was falling like a soft-bodied stone toward the earth. I was already on my feet and running.

The hare lay stunned, near death, its eyes

wide and yet unseeing. Its dusky fur was streaked with blood from the hawk's talons; I felt its labored breathing, its pain, the panic that went beyond fear. It blinked once, twice, and then its life began to ease away. "Sassen," I murmured, not touching it. Its little sides had quit heaving for breath. "Sassen," I said softly, tracing several sigils in the air above it, calling it back. "Sassen." I sang it coaxingly, and then the hare blinked, its eyes taking on a new awareness. It breathed deep, its velvet nose twitching. I watched as it rolled to its feet in a smooth movement and bounded off to the brush.

I know that some would say that what I did today is wrong, that it is interfering with nature's will, which should be held sacred. But I believe that as witches we should have the ability to use our own judgment. Nothing I have done today will throw off the balance of the universe: The hawk will catch more prey, the hare will die sooner or later. Both will go on with their lives, unaware of what I've done.

Animals are innocent. People never are.
—Justine Courceau

I told Da about helping the First Nation girl give birth. He seemed interested, his eyes on me, as he finished eating. I gave him the tiny piece of bread I had left, and he ate that, too, though it seemed to take effort.

"It sounds like you handled it well, son," he said in his odd, raspy voice. "Good for you."

My heart flared, and I became humiliatingly aware that part of me still longed to impress him. Impress *him,* this pale imitation of my father.

"Da," I began, leaning forward. "I need to talk to you about how you've been helping people around here. I'm a Seeker, and you must know that some of the things I've seen and heard concern me. I need to understand what you do, what role you play, how you've made it safe to be known openly as a witch."

For a moment I thought he might actually try to answer, but then he raised one hand in a defeated gesture and let it fall again. He glanced at me, gave a faintly embarrassed half smile, then stood and headed to his room, just like that.

I sat back in my chair, unreasonably stunned—why had I expected anything different? Maybe because when I was a child, my da had never turned away from answering a question, no matter how hard, how painful. He had given it to me straight, whether I really wanted the answer or not. I had to let go of that da—he was gone forever. In his place was this new man. He was what I had to work with.

That night I lay on the lumpy couch, unable to sleep and unwilling to do a calming spell until I had thought things through. I was a Seeker. Every instinct I had was on alert. I needed to find out what my father was up to. I needed some answers. If Da couldn't give them to me, I would find their answers myself. Then I would have a decision to make: whether to notify the International Council of Witches or not.

On Wednesday, I awoke early with renewed determination. I was going to follow Da today. All I had to do was wait for him to get up, then track him, something I was particularly good at.

Within moments of waking up, however, my senses told me the cabin was empty except for me. I frowned and swung my legs off the couch. A stronger scan revealed no other human around. How could that be? It would have been impossible for Da to wake and leave without my knowing. I was a light sleeper to begin with, and the couch of torture had only increased that. Then it occurred to me: it *was* impossible for Da to have left without my knowing. Which meant that my father had spelled me to keep me asleep. I sprang up, my hands clenching with anger. How dare he? He'd spelled me without my knowledge. There was no excuse for that, and it only emphasized how shady his business must be.

Swearing to myself, I shoved my feet into my boots and tied them with jerky movements. I pulled on the flannel shirt I'd earned, grabbed my coat, and stomped outside.

Outside, I saw that it was still early, and the air smelled like coming snow. The big pile of black garbage bags filled a corner of the front yard, and the thin, half-melted snow was tracked with my footprints. There were no tracks leading away from the house; none headed into the woods. Obviously Da had covered his trail.

I stomped a small circle into the snow and stepped into

it. It took several minutes for me to release my anger, to summon patience, to center myself and open myself to the universe. At last I was in a decent state, and I began to craft revealing spells.

I had to say this for him, Da still knew his spells. His concealing spells were in several layers and included some variations that took work and thought on my part to break through. Either he was a naturally gifted and innovative spell-crafter, or he had considered me a real threat. Or both.

When I was done, I felt cold and drained and wanted nothing more than a cup of tea and a warm fire. Instead I got up and retraced my steps around the cabin. I saw the repeated tracks of my feet leading to the woodpile, but this time I also saw a set of new footprints, one that definitely hadn't been there earlier: tracks leading from a corner of the porch into the woods. My mouth set in a firm line, I followed them.

How had my emaciated, malnourished father been able to hike this far the last couple of days, I wondered some forty minutes later. Granted, it was taking me longer because the tracks doubled back on themselves, I had to clear away other concealing and illusion spells, and I had to watch out for traps—but still, it had to be something desperately important to compel Da to trek this far every day in his weakened state.

A few minutes more and I became aware of a growing uneasiness, a bad taste in my mouth. I felt nervous; the back of my neck was tingling; all my senses were on alert. It was unnatural for the forest to be this quiet, this still. There were no animals, no birds, no movement or life of any kind. Instead a feeling of dread and disturbing silence pervaded the area. If I hadn't been on a mission, if I hadn't known I was tracking a witch—my father—I would have fled. Again and again, every minute, my senses told me to bolt, to get the hell out of there, to run as fast as I could through the thick forest, to not stop until I was home. It took all my self-control to ignore them, to push those feelings ruthlessly down. Goddess, what had he done?

I pressed forward and came at last to a smallish clearing. To one side of the clearing stood an old, round-roofed hut, made of sticks and covered with big strips of birch bark, like an Indian house. A fire burned unenthusiastically outside the hut. It was surrounded by huge logs, easily two feet in diameter, that looked like benches.

I felt ill. Nausea rose in my throat; my skin felt clammy, cold, and damp with sweat. From the strong pulls on my senses I could tell I was at a huge power sink, much like the one in the cemetery in Widow's Vale. But this one was made up of crossed lines, light and dark—it would be easy to work dark magick here, I realized, and my heart clenched.

I approached the hut. Every sense in me was screaming for me to get away from this place, to leave, that I was about to die, that I was suffocating. Dimly I was able to understand that these feelings were the effects of spells designed to ward off anyone who stumbled upon this place by accident, and I forced myself to ignore them. Taking a deep breath, I ducked down and pushed myself into the hut through its low doorway.

Immediately I was assaulted with feelings of out-and-out terror. My mouth went dry; my eyes were wild; my breath caught in my throat. Fighting for control, I looked around the hut with magesight. There was Da, crouched on the floor in a deep trance, his face alight with an unearthly eagerness. He was leaning over a dark . . . hole? Then it came to me, and my throat closed as if a fist were squeezing my windpipe shut. Dear Goddess. I had never seen one of these before, though of course I had read about them. My father was in front of a bith dearc, a literal opening into the netherworld, the world of the dead. My brain scrambled to understand, but nothing came to me except a horrified recognition. A bith dearc . . . if the council knew about this . . .

Da was oblivious to my presence, deeply entrenched in the shadow world. The atmosphere inside the hut was wretched, oppressive. I was reeling from shock and horror, wondering with panic how the hell this had become part of my life. Then, vaguely, my tortured senses picked up on the presence of a person outside. I stumbled back out through the opening, toward the clearing, to see a woman sitting on one of the log benches. She was poking listlessly at the fire with a stick, apparently used to having to wait and not seeming to feel the same terror and dread that was shredding my self-control.

I must have looked crazy, with my face white, my eyes wild, but she didn't seem to think anything of it, nor was she surprised to find someone here besides herself.

"*Bonjour,*" she said after a quick glance at me.

I sat down on a log across from her, my head between my knees so I wouldn't throw up. "*Bonjour,*" I muttered. I sucked in cold air, trying to clear my head, but the air here felt poisoned. How could my da be doing this? What to do, what to do?

"*C'est ma troisième visite à le sorcier,*" the woman confided.

It took me a moment to translate. Her third visit to the

witch. I wished I had thought to brush up on my French before I had come to this hateful place.

"Il m'aide de parler avec mon cher Jules," she went on, a stranger chatting in a doctor's waiting room. *"Jules mourut l'année dernière."*

My stomach roiled as I took in this information. My father helped this woman talk to her dear Jules, who died last year. Bloody hell. My father was helping people talk to their dearly departed. He had opened a bith dearc into the netherworld and was selling this service to his neighbors. It was appalling on so many levels, I didn't know what to react to first.

Apparently not bothered by my lack of response, the woman mused, *"Le sorcier, il est très compatissant. Le dernier fois, moi, je ne peut pas payer. Mais aujourd'hui, pour lui j'ai deux poules grosses."*

Great. My father was a prince. She couldn't pay last time, but today she had two nice chickens for him. My father was breaking some of the most seminal laws of the craft and being paid in chickens for it. I felt like I was losing my mind.

There had been times in history where it had been necessary, even imperative, to contact souls on the other side, times when it was sanctioned. But to commune with the dead on a regular basis, for payment—it was an affront to nature. It would never be allowed. This was exactly the kind of thing a Seeker would be sent to investigate, to shut down. This realization caused a sickening drop of my stomach.

Eventually, I wasn't sure how much later, Daniel came out, ashen faced. When he saw me sitting there, white with illness and misery, he staggered. His dull eyes went from me to the woman, who was still waiting patiently. Ignoring me, he went over to her and spoke gently to her in French, telling her today wasn't a good day, that she must return at another time. The look of utter disappointment on her face was heartbreaking. But she dutifully stood, offered my father her chickens, which he refused, smiling, and left. Leaving us alone, father and son, witch and Seeker.

9.
Fiona the Bright

I haven't heard a thing from Hunter, besides his phone message on Tuesday. (Why did he call while I was at school? Was he trying to not talk to me?) I'm starting to get worried. Either he's run into trouble and hasn't been able to contact anyone, or he's having a great time, doesn't want to come home, and hasn't been able to contact anyone. Either way, I'm scared.

I finally sent him a witch message last night, but I have no idea whether it reached him since I haven't heard anything back. It's getting harder and harder for me to concentrate on the rest of my life. I think about Hunter all the time. I think about last Friday night, how close we came, and wonder if we'll ever finally go all the way.

I went to Bethany's apartment yesterday after school. I'm comfortable with her. We talked some about healing herbs. I told her about the research I had done on-line, and she lent me one of her own books: A Healer's Herb Companion. I can't wait to get into it.

Bethany asked me about my plans for this year's garden, and I admitted I hadn't gotten far with them. She told me that she has a plot in the Ninth Street Community garden, two blocks from her apartment. Without being pushy or making me feel guilty, she helped me think about mine a little more, and now I'm excited all over again about my first one.

Right now, though, I would give anything to hear the phone ring. Hunter, where are you? What are you doing? Are you coming back to me?

—Morgan

"You've got to talk to me!" I shouted. My father turned away and paced into the kitchen, his shoulders stiff, his gaunt face set with anger.

I followed him, crossing the tiny lounge in four big paces. A bleak sunshine was trying to stream through the newly washed windows, but it was weak and seemed incapable of entering this house of darkness, death, and despair.

"How could you possibly think it's all right?" I demanded, pursuing him. Ever since we had gotten home, I had been trying to get answers from him. He had retreated into cold silence, regarding me as from a distance, as if I were nothing more than an annoying insect. I had spent most of the night awake, pacing in front of the fireplace, sitting on the couch, rubbing the back of my neck. Da had been in his room—if he slept, I didn't know it. I would bet he did. Nothing much seemed to get to him. Certainly not my revolted reaction to his bith dearc.

The next morning I jolted awake, slumped against the back of the couch, unaware of when I had fallen asleep. Our ugly fight started again. He looked, several times, as though he wanted to say something, to explain himself, but couldn't. I was alternately cajoling, supportive, angry, insistent. I never let down my guard, never left him alone.

Seeing him in the kitchen, hunting through the cabinets for something to eat, through food I had supplied, filled me with fresh anger. I had been here five days, five awful, disappointing, shocking days. I'd had enough.

"When I got here, you could hardly walk," I pointed out, coming closer. My anger was starting to spiral out of control, but for once I didn't rigidly clamp it down. "Now you're stronger because *I've* been taking care of you. And you're going out into the woods, to your bith dearc. Are you *mad?*"

Daniel turned and looked at me, his eyes narrowed. I almost wanted him to explode, to show me a side of my old father, any side, even anger. He paused, his hand on a cupboard shelf, then looked away.

"What would Alwyn say if she saw you, if she knew about this?" I demanded. "This is what killed her brother."

He looked at me, something flickering behind his dull brown eyes. Answer me, just answer me, I thought. "Please, stop," he said, sounding helpless. "You just don't understand."

"Explain it to me," I said, trying to calm down. "Explain why you've done this terrible thing."

"It *is* terrible," he agreed sadly. "I know that."

"Then why do you do it?" I asked. "How could you take payment for contacting the dead?"

We were face-to-face in that cramped kitchen. I was taller than he and outweighed him; I was a young, strong, healthy man, and he was a broken wreck far older than his years. But there was something latent in him, a reserve of ancient power lying coiled within him, awaiting his need for it. I sensed this; I'm not sure if he did.

His face twisted. "I have to," he said.

"It's making you ill. And you know it's wrong," I said, as if talking to a child. "Da, you've got to stop this."

His shoulders hunched, he looked away. Then, stiffly, as if holding back a cry, he nodded. "I know, lad. I know."

"Let me help you," I said, calming down more. "Just stay here today—don't go. I'll make you some lunch."

He gave another short nod and sat abruptly in his armchair, staring at the fire. His fingers twitched, a muscle in his jaw jumped—he looked like an addict facing withdrawal.

"Tell me about your town," Da said at lunch. It was the first question he had asked of me, the first interest he had shown in my life. I answered him, though I suspected he was only trying to change the subject.

"I've only been there about four months," I said, not mentioning the reason I had first gone there: to investigate his first wife, his first son. "But I've stayed and kept it my base in America. It's a little town, and it reminds me of England more than a lot of other American towns I've seen. It's kind of old-fashioned and quaint."

He bit into his BLT and almost looked like he enjoyed it for a second. Every once in a while he glanced at a window or the door, as if he would somehow escape if I let him. He was trying not to go to the bith dearc. He was trying to let me help him.

"Do you have a girl there?"

"Aye," I admitted, taking a huge bite of my own sandwich.

The thought of Morgan sent a tremor through my body. Goddess, I missed her.

"Who is she?"

"Her name is Morgan Rowlands," I said, wondering how to broach the topic of her parentage. "She's a blood witch, a Woodbane."

"Oh? Good or bad?" At his little joke he gave a small cough and took a sip of his juice.

"Good," I said wryly. How could I tell him what Morgan meant to me, who she was? That I believed she was my mùirn beatha dàn?

"What's her background? Tell me about her."

My pulse quickened. He sounded almost like a real father, the father I had always wanted. "She's amazing. She's only just found out about being a blood witch. But she's the strongest uninitiated witch I've ever seen or heard of. She's really special. I'd like you to meet her."

Da nodded with a vague smile. "Perhaps. How did she just find out about her powers? Who are her parents?"

My jaw tensed. I had no idea how my father would react to this. "Actually . . ."

Da looked up, sensing my hesitation. "What is it, lad?"

I sighed. "The truth is, she's the biological child of Maeve Riordan of Belwicket . . . and Ciaran MacEwan. Of Amyranth."

All expression seemed to drain from Da's face. "Really."

"Yes. But she was put up for adoption. . . . It's a long story, but Ciaran killed her mother, and Morgan just learned the truth about her heritage recently. She was adopted by a Catholic family in Widow's Vale."

My da's eyes flicked up at me. They were full of suspicion.

My father had been fleeing Amyranth and their destruction for eleven years, and now his son was involved with the leader's daughter. It had to be hard to take. "Does she . . . has she met Ciaran?"

"Yes," I admitted, remembering Ciaran's odd recent reunion with his daughter. "But she's very different from him. She wants to work for good, like her mother worked for good. She helped the council find him. You know that he's in custody now."

Da nodded and went on eating. I had no idea what he was thinking.

"Did you know Cal?" he asked.

My jaw almost dropped. When I was young, Selene and Cal were never, ever mentioned in our house. In fact, I hadn't found out about them until right before I had come to Widow's Vale. I still remember how stunned I had been by the news.

"Only a bit," I said.

Da put down his sandwich, took a sip of beer. "What was he like?"

He was a bloody criminal, I wanted to say, letting out my still white-hot anger at the person who almost destroyed Morgan. He was evil personified. But this was Da's son—my half brother. And I suppose, deep down, I knew that Cal hadn't really had a chance, not with Selene Belltower for a mother.

"Um. He was very good-looking," I said objectively. "He was very charismatic."

"You hated him." It was a statement.

"Yes."

"I don't know what I was thinking, leaving him with her," Da said, his voice dry and aged. "All I knew was I was in love with your mother; she'd already had you. I wanted to be with her. I didn't want Selene and her evil tendrils wrapping around my life. At the time, I told myself that a child that young should stay with his mother. And Selene always said there was no way I could take him from her. Ever. But now I wonder if I could have—if I'd tried hard enough. And I wonder if I didn't try because I hated Selene so much, I didn't want any part of her near me—not even our son."

Crikey. I'd never heard Da talk like this. It made him seem so much more human somehow.

"Well, anyway. Old days," he said blithely, seeming embarrassed to reveal so much. Yet it was just this that allowed me to get past my new vision of him—the disappointing father—and see him as the man I remembered. A good man, who had loved, made mistakes, had regrets. It was a side of him I liked.

"I'm knackered," he said, sounding shaky. He stood up and walked past me with hesitant steps. I followed him to his bedroom, where he lay down on clean sheets. I guessed that the pull of the bith dearc was still working on him.

"Da, let me help," I said, coming to stand by the side of the bed. He looked up at me with uncomprehending weariness, and gently I laid my fingers on his temple, the way I had with the First Nation girl. I sent waves of soothing calmness, feelings of safety, of relaxation. In moments his eyes had fluttered closed and his breathing changed to that of a man asleep. I stayed for a moment, making another spell of deep rest. If I could just keep him away from the bith dearc, if he would rest, I knew that I could help him get stronger. And perhaps then . . . when he was back to his old self . . . perhaps then I could get him away from this place, back home with me in Widow's Vale.

He would be out for hours, I figured, watching his sunken chest rise and fall. I went into the lounge, got my coat, and headed to town.

In town I was startled by how normal things seemed. I checked my watch—it was after three. Please be there, I thought, punching in my phone card number, then Morgan's number. Mary K.'s bright voice answered the phone.

"Hunter!" she said happily. "Where are you? Morgan's been so awful lately because she hasn't talked to you."

"I'm sorry," I said. "My mobile can't get a signal here, my father doesn't have a phone, and it's hard for me to get to town sometimes. Is she there? Can I speak to her?"

"No, she hasn't gotten home yet. Jaycee's mom gave me a ride from school. I don't know if Morgan's with Bree or what. You want Bree's cell phone number?"

"Yes, thanks. It's been too long since I talked to her."

"I know *she* thinks so," said Mary K. primly, and I smiled to myself, wondering how grumpy Morgan had been all week.

Mary K. gave me Bree's number, and I called it as soon as we hung up. But a recorded voice told me that the mobile customer I was calling was not available. I wanted to smash the phone receiver against the booth wall. Dammit. I needed to talk to Morgan, needed to hear her voice, her comforting, encouraging reactions to my horrible situation. I called Bree's cell phone again and left a message, asking her to tell Morgan that I had tried to call her and really missed her and hoped we could talk soon.

Next I tried calling Sky. I didn't even bother to calculate what time it would be in France—I needed to hear a semi-friendly voice. No one was home. I was starting to feel desperate. Talking to my father was full of emotional highs and lows. I needed some medium.

In the end I talked to Kennet. Kennet had been my mentor, had taught me much about being a Seeker. But I didn't mention any of my fears about Da, didn't talk about the bith dearc or Da's transgressions. Kennet, however, had news for me.

"It's convenient you're up there, actually," he said.

I leaned into the phone booth, watching my breath come out in little puffs. "Yeah? Why's that?"

"The council has a job for you to do," he said.

"All right," I said with unusual eagerness. Anything to take my mind off the situation with my father. "Tell me what's going on."

"About three hours west from where you are, a Rowan-wand witch named Justine Courceau is collecting the true names of things."

"Yes?" I said, meaning, so what? Most witches make a point of learning as many true names of things as they can.

"Not just things. Living creatures. People. She's writing them down," said Kennet.

I frowned. "Writing them down? You have knowledge of this?" The idea of a witch compiling a list of the true names of living creatures, especially people, was almost unthinkable. Knowing something's true name gives one ultimate power over it. In some cases this is useful, even necessary; for example, in healing. But it is all too easy to misuse someone's true name, to use it for power's sake. Writing this information down would give that power to anyone who read the list. And knowing the true name of a human or witch would give someone ultimate power over them. It was very, very difficult to come by someone's true name. How had she been gathering them?

"Yes, she doesn't deny it," Kennet said. "We've sent her a letter, demanding she stop, going over some of the basic protocols of craft knowledge, but she hasn't responded. We'd like you to go see her, investigate the matter, and determine a course of action."

"No problem," I said, thinking about how relieved I would be to get away from here, if only for a short while.

"If it's true that she's keeping a list, then she must be stopped and the list destroyed," Kennet went on. "For such a list to fall into the wrong hands would be disastrous, and this Justine Courceau must be made to realize that."

"I understand. Can you tell me where she lives?"

Kennet gave me directions, and I fetched the map from the car and traced the route, making sure I understood. She lived in Ontario Province, near a town called Foxton. It appeared to be about three hours' drive from Saint Jérôme du Lac.

When I rang off with Kennet, it was almost dark. I stopped in at the grocer's to get more milk and more apples, feeling the irony of wanting to feed Da and yet resenting the fact that it gave him the strength he needed to get to the bith dearc. But I felt we had made real progress today. He had stayed away from the bith dearc. We had talked, really talked, for the first time. I hoped it was just the first step.

However, when I got back, the cabin was empty, the fire

burning unbanked in the fireplace. I knew immediately where he had gone. As fast as that, my anger erupted afresh, and in the next second I had thrown the groceries across the kitchen, seeing the container of milk burst against the wall, the white milk running down in streams. This wasn't me—I had always been self-control personified. What was happening to me in this place?

This time it took only twenty-five minutes to get to the hut, despite the fact that the path was still spelled and it was dark outside. My anger propelled me forward, my long legs striding through the woods as if it were daylight. The closer I got to the hut, the more I was assaulted by waves of panic and nausea. When I could hardly bear the feelings of dread, I knew I was close. And then I was in the clearing, the moonlight shining down on me, witnessing my shame, my anger.

Without hesitation I stormed into the hut, ducking through the low doorway, to find Daniel crouched over the eerily black bith dearc. He looked up when I came in, but this time his face was excited, glad. He flung out his hand to me.

"Hunter!" he said, and it struck me that this was perhaps the first time he had used my given name. "Hunter, I'm close, so close! This time I'll get through, I know it."

"Leave off this!" I cried. "You know this is wrong; you know this is sapping your strength. It's not good, it's not right; you know Mum would have hated this!"

"No, no, son," Da said eagerly. "No, your mum loved me; she wants to speak to me; she pines for me as I pine for her. Hunter, I'm close, so close this time, but I'm weak. With your help I know I could get through, speak to your mother. Please, son, just this once. Lend me your strength."

I stared at him, appalled. So this was what the bith dearc had *really* been about. Not helping others—that was incidental. His true goal had always been to contact Mum. But what he was suggesting was unthinkable, going not only against the written and unwritten laws of the craft, but also against my vows to the council as a Seeker.

"Son," Da said, his voice raspy and seductive. "This is your mother, your *mother,* Hunter. You know you were her favorite, her firstborn. She died without seeing you again, and it broke her heart. Give her the chance to see you now, see you one last time."

My breath left my lungs in a whoosh; Da's low blow had caught me unaware, and I almost doubled over with the pain of it. He was wily, Daniel Niall, he was ruthless. He had seen the chink in my armor and had rammed his knife home. It was a mistake for anyone to discount him as weak, as helpless.

"It's a powerful magick, Hunter," he wheedled. "Good magick to know, to be master of."

I snorted, knowing that anyone who thought he was master of a bith dearc was telling himself dangerous lies. It was like an alcoholic insisting he could stop anytime he wanted.

"It's your mother, son," said Daniel again.

Oh, Goddess. The reality of this opportunity suddenly sank in with a power that was all too seductive. Fiona . . . I had missed seeing my mother by two short months. To see her now—one last time—to feel her presence . . . Fiona the Bright, dancing around a maypole, laughing.

I sank to my knees across from my father, on the opposite side of the bith dearc. I felt sick and weakened; I was angry and embarrassed at my own weakness, angry at Da for being able to seduce me to his dark purpose. Yet if I could see my mother, just once . . . I knew how he felt.

Da reached out and put his bony hands on my shoulders. I did the same, clasping his shoulders in my hands. The bith dearc roiled between us, a frightening rip in the world, an oddly glowing black hole. Then together, with Daniel leading, we began the series of chants that would take us through to the other side.

The chants were long and complicated; I had learned them, of course: they were part of the basic knowledge I had to prove before I could be initiated. But naturally, I had never used them and had forgotten them in places. Then Daniel sang, his voice cracked and ruined, and I followed as best I could, feeling ashamed for my weakness and his.

I don't know how long we knelt there on the frozen ground, but gradually, gradually I began to become aware of something else, another presence.

It was my mother.

Though I hadn't seen or spoken to her in eleven years, there was no mistaking the way her soul felt, touching mine. I glanced up in awe to look at Daniel and saw that tears of joy were streaming down his hollowed cheeks. Then I realized that my mother's spirit had joined us in the hut. I could sense her shimmering presence, floating before us.

"At last, at last," came Da's whisper, like sandpaper.

I was scared, my mouth dry. I was not master of this magick, and neither was Daniel. This was wrong, it was trouble, and I should have had no part of it. This was how my brother had died, calling on dark magick to find a taibhs that had turned on him and taken his life.

"Hunter, darling." I felt rather than heard her voice.

"Mum," I whispered back. I couldn't believe that after eleven years, I was near her again, feeling her spirit.

"Darling, is it you?" Unlike Da, Mum seemed genuinely happy to see me, genuinely full of love for me. From her spirit I received waves of love and comfort, welcome and regret—more emotion than my father had spared for me so far. "Oh, Giomanach—you're a man, a man before my eyes," my mother said, her pride and wonder palpable. I started crying.

"My sweet, no," came her voice inside my head. "Don't spoil this with sadness. Let's take joy from this one chance to express our love. For I do love you, my son, I love you more than I can say. In life I was far from you; you were beyond my reach. Now nothing is. Now I can be with you, always, wherever you are. You need never miss me again."

I've never been comfortable with crying, but this was all too much for me—the pain of my last five days, my fear and worry for my father, my anger, and now this, seeing and hearing my long-lost mother, having her confirm what I thought I would wonder about my whole life: that she loved me, that she'd missed me, that she was proud of me, of who I had become.

"Fiona, my love, you've come back to me," said Da, weeping openly.

"No, my darling," said Mum gently. "You've called me here, but you know it can't be. I am where I am now and must stay. And you must stay in your world, until we can be together again."

"We can be together now!" my father said. "I can keep the bith dearc open; we can be together."

"No," I said, pulling myself back to reality. "The bith

dearc is wrong. You have to shut it down. If you don't, I will."

His eyes blazed at me. "How can you say that? It's given you your mother back!"

"She's not back, Da," I said. "It's her spirit; it isn't her. And she can't stay. And you can't make her. This isn't good for her, and it's going to kill you."

Angrily my father started to say something, but my mother intervened. "Hunter's right, Maghach," she said, a slight edge to her voice. "This isn't right for either of us."

"It is. It could be," Da insisted.

"Hunter is thinking more clearly than you, my love," Mum said. "I am here this once. I can't come here again."

"You must come back," my father said, a note of desperation entering his voice. "I must be with you. Nothing is worthwhile without you."

"Be ashamed, Maghach," my mother said in her no-nonsense tone. It gave me joy to hear it, bringing back memories of my childhood, when I'd had parents. "To say that nothing is worthwhile dishonors the beauty of the world, the joy of the Goddess."

"If you can't stay, then I'll kill myself!" Daniel said wildly, his hands reaching for her spirit. "I'll kill myself to be with you!"

My mother's face softened, even as I despised the weakness my father was showing. "My darling," she said gently. "I love you with all my heart. I always did, from the first moment I saw you. I look forward to loving you again, in our next lives together, and again, in our lives after that. You will always be the one for me. But now I am dead, and you are not, and you mustn't desecrate the Goddess by wishing to be dead yourself. To deny life is wrong. To mourn in a negative, self-centered way is wrong. You must live for yourself, and for your children. Hunter and Alwyn need your help and your love."

I was glad to hear my mother confirm the feelings I'd had about this. I felt a mixture of pathos and disgust, pity and shame, watching the despair on Da's face.

"I don't care!" he cried, and I wanted to hate him. "All I want is to be with you! You are my life! My breath, my soul, my happiness, my sanity! Without you there is nothing. Don't you understand?" My father fell forward onto his arms, sobs shaking his thin frame. Once again I felt this couldn't be the father I had known. I was horrified at how weak he had become.

"Don't judge him too harshly, Hunter," came Mum's voice, and I sensed she was speaking to me alone. "When you were a child, he was a god to you, but now you see that he's just a man, and he's mourning. Don't judge him until you too have lost something precious."

"I did lose something precious," I said, looking in her direction. "I lost my brother. I lost my parents."

Her voice was sad and regretful. "I'm so sorry, my love. We did what we thought was best. Perhaps we were wrong. I know you've suffered. And Linden suffered, too, perhaps most of all. But that wasn't your fault; you know that. And please believe me when I say that I loved you, Linden, and Alwyn with every breath, every second of every day. I made you, I bore you, and I will be with you forever."

I hung my head, unwilling to start crying again.

"My son," she said, "please take your father away from here. Destroy this bith dearc. Don't let Daniel return. My shadow world will eventually sap his strength and take his life if he doesn't stay away. And if he keeps calling me back, my spirit will be unable to progress on its journey. As much as I love your father, you, and Alwyn, I know that it's right for my spirit to move on, to see what more lies ahead of me."

"I understand," I choked out. My father was still bent double, weeping. I felt something brush me, as if Mum had touched me with her hand, and as she faded away, I saw a flash of her beautiful face.

"Fiona! No!" Da cried, reaching futilely for her, then collapsing again. When she was gone, I swallowed hard and rubbed the sleeve of my shirt against my face. Then, getting to my feet, I grabbed hold of my father's arm and dragged him outside, into the cold air. As awful as it was outside, it was still better than the wretched sickness of the hut.

Daniel crumpled to the ground, and I stumbled, trying to catch him. I felt weak, light-headed, and sick, as if someone had dosed me with poison. At first I didn't understand why I felt so terrible, but then I realized that Mum had meant her words literally: contacting the shadow world saps one's life force. I looked at my father, facedown on the ground, clawing at the snow-encrusted dirt, and realized exactly why Daniel looked so awful—who knew how long he'd been doing this? Two months? It was a wonder he was alive at all, if I felt like this after only one time, and I was a young, strong, healthy man.

It came to me that I might have to turn Daniel in to the council to save his life. I wondered whether I would have the strength. I staggered to my feet and pulled my father up by one arm. Then, with him leaning heavily on me, we headed back to the cabin.

10.
Shadows

There is somebody coming.

I first became aware of it this morning as I tried to concentrate on my work down in the library. I had laid out the salt, I had lit the candles, and I felt like I had been chanting for hours but to no avail. I wasn't breaking through. My shadow friends seemed hesitant to meet me. It was almost as if they were afraid—of something or somebody. I went upstairs to scry, and there I had my vision. A Seeker, coming here. I had a vague sense of youth, of emotional turmoil. Whoever this Seeker is, I do not fear him. He has his own troubles. He will not sway me from my life's work.

On Wednesday, I made an amazing breakthrough. I have developed a host of friends in the shadow world—many of them fellow

Rowanwands who see the value of my research and are eager to help. One of these friends, an older man who will only give the name Bearnard, brought to me a new and eager associate, a woman who calls herself Naible and who brought with her a wealth of knowledge. Never before have I come across anyone—in the living world or the shadow world—who has such an extensive knowledge of true names as this woman. From her I obtained nearly twenty true names that day, and she has promised to return with more knowledge, more names. Oh, Goddess, I have only gratitude for this generous woman and her love of knowledge. I wish that I had known her while she was among the living; what a remarkable team we would have made.

The Seeker is coming, and once he arrives, I will not be able to continue my research until he is gone. Goddess, give me the courage to remember my objectives and the intelligence to prevent this Seeker from truly learning what I seek. If only Naible could give me the true name of this Seeker . . . then he would stand no chance against me.

—J. C.

On Sunday, I woke up to find my father's bed empty. Hell! I had been right: it was like living with a junkie, and I always had to be on alert in case he tried to score. I immediately threw on some clothes, feeling a mixture of anger, a reluctant empathy, and a tight impatience.

It was amazing what desperation could lead a man to do, I thought twenty minutes later. My father was so weak that a trip to the grocery store could exhaust him for hours, but here, in his overwhelming desire to reach his bith dearc, he was able to trudge for miles through a Canadian forest in winter.

As I neared the place of darkness, feeling the familiar senses of nausea and fear, I wondered bleakly what I was going to do with my father—let him kill himself? Try to save him? Steeling myself, drawing on any strength I had, I ducked into the low opening of the hut and found my father, his face lighting with ecstasy. As my eyes focused, I felt my mother's spirit take shape above the glowing opening into the shadow world. Daniel looked up, joy making him seem twenty years younger. He reached out his hands to her ethereal form.

I crept close, awed by my mother's presence as I had been the first time. Kneeling by Daniel, I couldn't help allowing myself to enjoy the feel of her presence, which would be all I could have until I joined her one day in the shadow world.

"Daniel," Mum said, "I'm telling you that you must stop this. You must remain among the living. It is not your time." Her voice sounded more firm, and I was glad. If she had been truly needy or welcoming, Da would have been dead a month ago.

"I don't know how, Fi," Da answered, shaking his head. "I only know how to be with you."

"That isn't true," my mother said. "You had a lifetime of

other people before me." I felt a warmth from her directed at me, almost like a smile, and I smiled back, though I was feeling queasy and weakened by the bith dearc.

"I don't want other people," Da said stubbornly.

"You will learn to want other people," Mum said firmly, taking on a tone that was so familiar to me—the one she took when one of us kids had persisted too long in lame excuses for a wrongdoing. "Now I'm telling you, Daniel, you must not call me back again. You are hurting me. My spirit must move on. You're not letting that happen. Do you want to hurt me?"

"Goddess, Fiona, no!" said my father, looking appalled.

My mother's voice softened. "Daniel, you were the strong one in our marriage. You kept us going when I would have given up. It was your strength I relied on. I need to rely on that strength now. You must be strong enough not to call me back, to stay with the living. Do you understand?"

Da looked at the ground, seeming lost, bereft. Finally he gave a broken nod and covered his face with his hands.

Once again I felt the warmth from my mother, but tinged with sadness—a sadness borne of understanding and empathy. She knew how much my father was suffering; she knew how much I had suffered. She loved us both with all her heart, and in return I felt an intense love for her, the mother I had lost.

Silently Fiona's spirit brushed a shadowy kiss across us both, and floated through the bith dearc. As soon as she was gone, my father collapsed on his side on the ground. I sagged myself, hating the feeling of weakness and sickness that pulled me down. But I struggled to sit up and quickly performed the rite that would shut the bith dearc down. When the last of it had faded and I could see solid, frozen ground again, I sat back, trying not to throw up.

As soon as I could, I got Da out of there, and again we sank down outside in the snow, too weak to move. Ten minutes later I felt together enough to call to my da, who was lying, gray faced, on the ground a few feet away from me.

"I can't believe you!" I said, letting fly with my frustration. "Could you possibly be more stupid, more self-destructive? Could you be a little more selfish?"

Da's eyes fluttered open, and he sat up slowly, with difficulty. If he had been the old da, he would have come over and backhanded me. But this da was weak, in mind, body, and spirit.

"Why are you choosing death over being with your live children?" I went on, feeling my anger ignite. "I'm the only son you have left! Alwyn's the only daughter you'll ever have! You don't think you should stick around for our sakes? Not only that, but you're deliberately hurting Mum. Every time you contact her, every time you draw her to the bith dearc, you're slowing down her spirit's progress. She needs to move on. She must go on to the next phase of her existence. But you don't give a bloody flip! Because you can only think about *yourself*!"

Da's eyes were focused intently on me now, and his ashen cheeks were splotched pale red with anger. "I've tried to resist—" he began, but I cut him off.

"You haven't tried bloody hard enough!" I shouted, getting to my feet. My stomach roiled, but I stood, looming over him like a bully. "You just keep giving in! Is that what you want to teach me, your son? You want to teach me how to give in, give up, think only about myself? That's what you're showing me. You never would have been this way eleven years ago. Back then you were a real father. Back then you were a real witch. Now look at you," I concluded bitterly. I could count on one hand the number of times I had been this hateful, this mean to someone I cared about. I hated the words coming out of my mouth but couldn't stop them once I started.

"You have no idea how hard it is," my father said, his voice scraped raw.

I snorted and paced around the spent fire in the middle of the log benches. I felt ill, exhausted; I needed to get out of there. I knew I had to bring Da back to the cabin, but I had to talk myself out of leaving him there to freeze. Minutes passed, and I wondered what the hell I was going to do with myself. Everything in my life right now was miserable. The only person who could make me feel at all better wasn't here, and I couldn't seem to reach her. Bloody hell, why did I ever come here?

At last, after a long time, Da said, "You're right." He sounded impossibly old and broken down.

I looked over at him, and he went on, struggling to find the words.

"You're right. I'm being selfish, thinking only of myself. Your mother would have been stronger. She should have been the one to live."

My eyes narrowed as I readied to nip his self-pity in the bud.

"But it was me that lived, and I'm making a hash of it,

aren't I, lad?" He gave a crooked, fleeting smile, then looked away. "It's just—I can't let her go, son. She was my life. I gave up my firstborn son for her."

I gave a short nod. Cal.

"And then," he went on, "for the past eleven years it's been only me and Fiona, Fiona and me, everywhere we went, every day. We were alone; we didn't dare make friends; we went for months without seeing another human, much less another witch. I don't even know how to be with other people anymore."

I looked away and let out a long breath. When Da sounded like this, somewhat rational, somewhat familiar, it was impossible to hold on to my anger. Mum had reminded me that he was just a man, in mourning for his wife, and I needed to cut him a huge swath of slack.

I raised my hands and let them fall. "Da, you could learn how—"

"Maybe I could," he said. "I guess I'll have to. But right now there's no way I can give up the bith dearc, no way I can give up Fiona. The only thing that will stop me is to be stripped of my powers. If I have no power, I can't make a bith dearc; I won't be able to. So that's what I need from you. You're a Seeker; you know how. Take my powers from me, and save me from myself."

My eyebrows rose, and I searched his eyes, hoping to find any trace of sanity left. Was he joking about such a terrible thing? "Have you ever seen anyone stripped of their powers?" I asked. "Do you have any idea how incredibly horrible it is, how painful, how you feel as though your very soul has been ripped from you?"

"It would be better than this!" Da said, his voice stronger. "Better than this half existence. It's the only way. As long as I have power, I'll be drawn to the bith dearc."

"That's not true!" I said, pacing again. "It's been only two months. You need more time to heal—anyone would. We just need to come up with a plan, that's all. We need to think."

He made no answer but allowed me to pull him to his feet. It took almost forty minutes for us to get back to the cabin, with our slow, awkward pace. Inside, I stoked up a fire. A dense chill permeated my bones, and I felt like I would never get rid of it. Keeping my coat on, I lowered myself to the couch. Da was sitting, small and gray and crumpled, in his chair. I felt exhausted, ill, near tears. Frustrated, pained, joyful at seeing my mother. Horrified and shocked at my father's demand that I strip him of his powers. I had too many emotions inside me. Too many to name, too many to express. I was so overwhelmed that I felt numb. Where to start? All at once I felt like a nine-teen-year-old kid—not like a mighty Seeker, not like the older, more experienced witch that Morgan saw me as. Not like an equal, like Alyce felt. Just a kid, without any answers.

Finally I just started talking, my head resting against the back of the couch, my eyes closed. "Mum was right, you know," I said without accusation. His request that I strip him of his powers had blown my anger apart. "I under-stand how you felt about her, I really do. She was your mùirn beatha dàn, your other half. You only get the one, and now she's gone. But you were a whole person before you met Mum, and you can be a whole person now that she's gone."

My father kept silent.

"I don't know how I would feel if I lost my mùirn beatha dàn," I said, thinking of Morgan, the unbelievable horror of Morgan being dead. "I can't really say if I would have the strength to behave any differently. I just don't know. But surely you can see how this is going down the dark path. Ignoring life in favor of death isn't something you would have taught us kids. This is the path that killed Linden. But two of your children are still alive, and we need you." Looking at him, I saw his shoulders shake, perhaps with just exhaustion.

I made up my mind. The council wanted me to head west, to go interview Justine Courceau. I decided to take Da with me, whether he wanted to go or not. Mum was right— if Da stayed here, he would keep using the bith dearc and eventually kill himself. It wasn't a great plan, a long-term fix, but it was all I had.

Standing up, I went and threw clothes for both of us into a duffel. Da didn't look up, showed no interest. I made tea, packed some food and drinks for the three-hour drive, and loaded the car. Then I knelt by his chair, looking up at him.

"Da. I need to go west for a few days on council business. You're going with me," I said.

"No," he weakly, not looking up. "That's impossible. I need to rest. I'm staying here."

"Sorry—can't let you do that. You'll end up killing yourself. You're coming with me."

In the old days, Da could have lifted me up and thrown me like a sack of potatoes. These days, I was the strong one. In the end, pathetically, he didn't have much choice.

Half an hour later he was buckled into the front seat next to me, his mouth set in a defeated line, his hands twitching at the knees of his corduroys, as if waiting for the day when he would be strong enough to fasten them around my neck. I had no idea whether that day would ever come, whether my da would ever resemble the father I had known before. All I knew was that we were headed for Foxton, a small town in Ontario, and after my job there was done—I didn't know what I was going to do.

Justine Courceau lived at the very edge of the Quebec-Ontario province border. I endured three and a half hours of stony silence on the way. Fortunately the scenery was incredible: rocky, hilly, full of small rivers and lakes. In springtime it would be stunning, but here, at the tail end of winter, it still had a striking and imposing beauty.

The small town Kennet had directed me to, Foxton, had one bed-and-breakfast. First I got Da and me settled there and brought up our lone duffel. Da seemed completely spent, his face cloud-colored, his hands shaky, and he seemed relieved enough to curl up on one of the twin beds in our room. I felt both guilty and angry about his misery. Since he seemed dead asleep, I performed a few quick healing spells, not knowing whether they were strong enough to have any effect on a man in my da's condition. Then I put a watch sigil on one of his shoes, figuring he couldn't go anywhere without it and that he would be less likely to feel it than if it was on his body. This way I could stay in contact with him, be more or less aware of what he was doing, be aware if he tried to do something stupid, like harm himself. Then I grabbed my coat and car keys and locked the door behind me. Regretting it, I spelled the door so it would be hard for him to get out. In any other circumstance, such a thing would be unthinkable, but I didn't trust Da to be making the best decisions right now.

This was never how I'd thought I'd be using my magick. It left a bad taste in my mouth.

Kennet had told me Justine Courceau was a Rowanwand, and I had to deliberately put aside my personal feelings about the clan before I got to her house. Frankly, I've often found Rowanwands to be rather full of themselves. They make such a production of their dedication to good, of their fight against dark, evil Woodbanes. It just seems a bit much.

Kennet had been able to give me very accurate directions, and barely twenty minutes after I had left Da, I was bumping down a long driveway bordered on both sides with hardwoods: oaks, maples, hickorys. It was a pretty spot, and again I imagined how it would look in springtime. I hoped I wouldn't be here to see it.

After about a quarter mile, the driveway stopped in front of a cottage that to my eyes screamed "witch." It was small, picturesque, and made of local stone. Surrounding it was the winter version of a garden that must, in summer, be astounding. Even now, dormant and dusted with snow, it was well tended, tidy, pleasing.

Before I left my car, I went through my usual preparations. When a Seeker approaches someone she or he is investigating, anything can happen. An unprepared Seeker can soon be a dead Seeker. I took a moment to focus my thoughts, sharpen different defenses, physical and magickal, that were in place, and did the usual ward-evil, protection, and clarity spells. At last I felt sufficiently Seekerish, and I got out of my car and locked it.

I walked up a meandering stone path toward the bright red front door, wondering what Ms. Courceau would be like. Judging by the cottage, I was already picturing her as something like Alyce, perhaps. Gentle, kindly, with three or four cats. I hoped it would be as easy as it seemed. Unfortunately, I've learned that isn't always the case.

While I had been sitting in my car, no face had peered out through the thick-paned, old-fashioned windows, bordered with dark green shutters, and I hoped Ms. Courceau was home. I didn't see a car. Glancing toward the back, I saw a small greenhouse attached to the cottage, plus quite a few well-ordered squares of garden behind. Maybe there was a garage back there as well.

At the front door I put all my senses on alert and rapped the shining brass door knocker. I felt someone casting their senses toward me and instinctively blocked them. The door opened hesitantly, and a woman stepped forward. I was momentarily taken aback.

"Justine Courceau?" I asked.

She nodded. "Yes. Can I help you?"

My first, instantaneous impression was that she was much younger than I had assumed. I realized Kennet hadn't mentioned her age, but this woman couldn't have been more than twenty-two or twenty-three. She was strikingly pretty, with shoulder-length dark red hair. Her skin was clear and ivory toned, and her eyes were wide and brown, kind of like Mary K.'s.

"I'm Hunter Niall," I said. "The council sent me here to talk to you." This sentence can create any number of different reactions, from defiance, to fear, to curiosity or confusion. This was the first time someone had laughed at me outright.

"I'm sorry," Justine said, stifling her laughter but still smiling widely. "Goodness. A Seeker? I had no idea I was so scary. Come in and have some tea. You must be frozen."

Inside, her cottage was charming. I cast my senses and picked up on nothing but the usual frissons of lingering magick, regular magick—nothing odd or out of place. I detected faint traces of mild spellcraft, the pleasing scents of herbs and oil, and a quiet sense of joy and accomplishment. I could feel nothing dark, nothing that set off my radar. Instead I felt more comfortable in this room than I had in most of the places I had been in the last six months.

"Please, sit down," said Justine, and I processed the musical notes of her voice, wondering if she sang. "The kettle's already on—I won't be half a minute." She spoke perfect English but with a soft French accent. I was just glad she spoke English. It would have been hard going, doing all this in French.

The sofa in the lounge was oversized, chintz covered, and comfortably worn. On the table before it rested a circular arrangement of pine cones, dried winter berries, some pressed oak leaves. It was unpretentious and artistic, and the whole cottage struck me that way. I wondered if this was all her taste or whether she had lived here with her parents and then inherited all their decor.

As soon as I sank onto the couch, two cats of undistinguished breed approached me and determinedly climbed into my lap, curling up, kneading my legs with their paws, trying to both fit into a limited space. I stroked their soft, winter-thick fur and again picked up nothing except well-fed contentment, health, safety.

"Here we go," said Justine, coming in with a laden tea tray. There was a pot of steaming Darjeeling tea, some sliced cake, some fruit, and a small plate of cut sandwiches. After the past week of my doing all the cooking, it was nice to have someone feed me for a change.

Holding my tea over the cats on my lap, I said, "Obviously you know why I'm here. The council sent you a letter that you didn't respond to. Do you want to tell me what's going on, in your own words?"

Her brown eyes regarded me frankly over her Belleek teacup. "Now that I look at you, you seem quite young for a Seeker. Is this your first job?"

"No," I said, unable to keep the weariness out of my voice. "Do you want to tell me what's going on, in your own words?" Witches tended to prevaricate and avoid a Seeker's questions. I had seen it before.

"Well," she said thoughtfully, "I assume you're here because I collect the true names of things." She took a sip of tea, then curled one leg underneath her on her chair.

"Yes. Every witch uses them to some degree, but I hear you're collecting the names of living beings and writing them down. Is that true?"

"You know it's true," she said with easy humor, "or you wouldn't be here."

I took a bite of sandwich: cucumber and country butter on white bread. My mouth was very happy. I swallowed and looked up at her. "Talk to me, Ms. Courceau. Tell me what you're doing."

"Justine, please." She shrugged. "I collect the true names of things. I write them down because to learn and remember all of them would take me a lifetime. I don't do anything with them; I don't misuse them. It's knowledge. I'm Rowanwand. We gather knowledge. Of any kind. Of every kind. This is what I'm focusing on right now, but it's only one of many areas that interest me. Frankly, it doesn't seem like the council's business." She leaned back in her chair, and another cat leapt up on the back of it and rubbed its head against her red hair.

I was aware that there was, if not exactly a lie, then a half-truth in what she had just told me. I continued to question her, to explore her motives.

"Many clans gather knowledge," I said mildly, breaking off a piece of cake with my fingers. "It's the very nature of a witch to gather knowledge. As Feargus the Bright said, 'To know something is to shed light on darkness.' But it makes a difference what kind of knowledge you collect."

"But it doesn't, don't you see?" Justine asked earnestly, leaning forward. "Knowledge in and of itself cannot be inherently evil. It's only what a person chooses to do with that knowledge that makes it part of good or evil. Do we want to take the chance that something precious and beautiful will be lost forever? I don't have children. What if I never have children? How will I impart what I've learned? Who knows what later generations might be able to do with it? Knowledge is just knowledge: it's pure; it's neutral. I know that I won't misuse it; I know that what I'm doing is going to be hugely beneficial one day."

Again I had just the slightest twinge of something on the edge of my consciousness about what she had said, but I would look at it later. Anyway, I could see her point of view so far. Many witches would agree with her. It wasn't my job to agree or disagree with her.

We talked for another hour. Sometimes Justine pressed her beliefs, sometimes we just chatted, learning about each other, sizing each other up. At the end of my visit I knew that Justine was very bright, extremely well educated (which she would be: I had recognized her mother's name as one of the foremost modern scholars of the craft), funny, self-deprecating, and strong. She was wary; she didn't trust me any more than I trusted her. But she wanted to trust me; she wanted me to understand. I felt all that.

Finally, almost reluctantly, I needed to go. It had been a nice afternoon and such a great change from the hellish disappointment the last week had been. It was nice to talk to an ordinary witch instead of someone hell-bent on his own destruction, someone mired in grief and pain.

"I'd like to meet with you again before I make my report to the council," I said. I carefully dislodged the cats in my lap and stood, brushing fur off my jeans. Justine watched me with amusement, making no apologies.

"You're welcome here anytime," she said. "There aren't any other witches around here for me to talk to. It's nice to have company I can really be myself with." She had a nice smile, with full lips and straight white teeth. I put on my coat.

"Right, then, I'll be in touch," I said, opening the front door. As I started down the stone path, I became suddenly aware of Justine's strong interest in me. I was surprised; she hadn't given a sign of it inside. But now I felt it: her physical attraction to me, the fact that she liked me and felt comfortable with me. I didn't acknowledge it but got into my car, started the engine, and waved a casual good-bye.

11.
The Rowanwand

The Seeker arrived yesterday. I don't know how to describe my reaction—he's an invader, and I should resent his being here, yet he is so . . . interesting. He is an Englishman, young, scarcely even twenty. Yet he carries himself with a confidence, a maturity that makes me think he has great potential. I do sense turmoil in him—whether it is a result of this assignment or a personal problem, I can't say. Still, he is so attractive to me, so stimulating to talk to, I find myself wondering if I could win his heart.

Of course, I haven't been able to do any research since I sensed him coming. I've stripped the library of any traces of magick and have performed endless purification rituals to keep him from sensing the taint of the other side. I miss my work and my friends in the shadow *world more than I can express, but I can be patient. The Courceaus know much about patience, biding our time, waiting until the right moment to make our intentions known.*

Goddess, help me to keep my focus and remember that it is my work that is most important—more important than any temporary attraction I might have. If only there were some way to make him understand. If only I could get his true name . . .

—J. C.

This morning I spent time in Foxton proper, hanging out at the local bookstore, the coffee shop, the library. It's a bigger town than Saint Jérôme du Lac and has more resources. Basically I was casting my senses, trying to listen for gossip about Justine. Unlike my father, no one here seems to have identified her as a witch, though quite a few people knew who she was. I mentioned her name in a few places, and people had only good things to say about her. The previous autumn she'd led a fund drive for the library, and it had been their most successful ever. One woman told me how Justine had helped when her dog was ill—she'd been a godsend. The general impression was that she was something of a loner but friendly and helpful when needed. They thought of her as a good neighbor.

The way Kennet had talked about her, I had been prepared for another Selene Belltower—an amoral, ruthless user who felt she was above the council laws. Justine didn't seem that way at all. Though, of course, appearances can be deceiving.

Back at the bed-and-breakfast, Da was doing a lot of lying around, staring at the walls. I had brought several books to read, and I offered them to him. If he knew about the watch sigil or the spelled door, he didn't mention them. Mostly he seemed incredibly depressed, hopeless, uninterested in anything. I wanted to jolt him out of his stupor but wasn't sure how. I wished there was a healer around.

That afternoon Daniel lay down with a book, and I headed back to Justine's. She greeted me cheerfully, and soon I was again sitting in her comfortable lounge, with cats appearing out of nowhere to take naps on me.

"I've been thinking about what you said yesterday," she began. "About the council laws and why we have them. And I'm just not convinced. I mean, I obey all Canadian laws, and I recognize their right to have and enforce them. After all, I'm choosing to live here. If I don't like their laws, I can decide to move somewhere else. But I have no choice about being a witch. I *am* one, by blood. It would be impossible for me not to be one. So why should I accept the council's laws as valid over me? They set themselves up almost two hundred years ago. Nowadays they're elected, but the entire council, in and of itself, wasn't created by the Wiccan community or even by the Seven Clans. To me they seem arbitrary. Why should I subject myself to their laws?"

I leaned forward. "It's true that the council created itself long ago. But the original members were witches, just as all members are today. The council wasn't created by humans, who have nothing to do with witch affairs. The creation of the council signifies the intent of the witch community at large to be self-governing. And yes, we're all subject to whatever human laws govern the places in which we live, but those laws don't address the sum of our existence. Everyone who practices the craft, everyone who works with magick is a part of a different world. That world intersects with the human world but doesn't overlap." I adjusted one of the cats on my lap, whose claws were digging into my thigh. "We're not talking about golf here, Justine. We're talking about magick. You know as well as I do that magick can be incredibly powerful, life altering, dangerous, misused, destructive. You don't think it's a good idea to have some sort of mutually agreed-upon guidelines for it? Do you really think it would be preferable to have no laws in place? So that every witch could make any kind of magick she or he wants, with no fear of reprisal?"

Her brows came down in a thoughtful V, and she pulled a corner of one lip into her mouth: she was thinking. "It's just that the laws seem arbitrary," she argued, crossing her legs under her. Today she wore faded jeans and a fuzzy pink sweater that showed the neck of a white T-shirt underneath. She looked very fresh and pretty. "I mean, look at the rules about uninitiated witches making certain kinds of magick. Why does someone need some stranger's stamp of approval just to do what comes naturally? I hate that."

"But *what* comes naturally, Justine?" I asked. I was enjoying this back-and-forth discussion. I hardly ever got to have this kind of interesting, stimulating conversation. Among the witches I knew, we all just accepted the council's laws. And other people, like Morgan, don't really know enough about Wiccan history or the witch community to be able to fully form an opinion. "What kind of magick did you make as a child? That was natural, wasn't it? But was it always good?" I thought about my own spell on poor Mrs. Wilkie. "I don't believe either people or witches are always born naturally good," I went on. "I think that as people get older and more educated, they learn to channel their goodness, to identify it, and to express it. But I think witches, and people, too, are born with a capacity for light or dark. It's up to their parents, their community, their teachers to educate them to see the consistent benefit of good and the consistent detriment of darkness. The council and its laws only serve to reinforce that, to provide guidelines, to help people learn where the boundaries are."

"But is that all they do?" asked Justine, and we were off again. For the next hour we went back and forth, discussing the various merits of laws versus no laws, outer-determined behavior versus inner-determined behavior. It was really fun, though at times I was uncomfortably reminded of the scientists who had figured out how to make an atom bomb. They had seemed to divorce the idea of how to create it from the idea of what its natural consequences would be. They hadn't wanted to see it. In a way, I felt that Justine was doing the same thing: closing her eyes to the potentially destructive effects of her actions.

But we talked on. Justine was sure of herself, sure of her own intelligence and attractiveness, and didn't let insecurity get in the way of her speaking her mind. For a moment I wondered if I should be concerned that I was enjoying her company so much but then thought, Nah. I knew I loved Morgan more than anything. I was doing my job, being a Seeker, finding out what made Justine tick. It was all for the report.

I had talked to Morgan the night before, but it had been kind of stilted. Hearing her voice had brought back my unhappiness about my parents, about how much I missed Morgan herself, about how much I didn't want to be here. Widow's Vale seemed so far away from here, both physically and emotionally.

"I was wondering—are you interested in seeing my library?" Justine asked.

"Yes," I said immediately, aware that this was a show of trust on her part. For my part, a Seeker never turns down an invitation into someone's private world. It's often where I find the answers to my questions.

She led me through a tidy, well-stocked kitchen to a small door in a hallway. She passed her hands over the door frame: dispelling protection spells. Once opened, the door led to steps going downward. I immediately became alert and quickly cast my senses to see if anything unpleasant was waiting for me at the bottom of the stairs.

"It's underground," Justine explained, turning on the electric lights. She didn't seem to pick up on my momentary suspicion, or maybe she was just being polite. "That helps keep it safe from fire. I think the people who owned this house before me used the cellar as storage, as a wine cellar. I enlarged it and waterproofed it."

At the bottom of the stairs she flicked another light switch, and I blinked, looking around. Justine's library was enormous. We were in one good-sized room, but doorways led to at least two other rooms I could see. The floor was made of rough wooden planks, and the walls were a crude stucco. But most bare surfaces had been painted with stylized designs of runes, hexes, words, and even some sigils I didn't know the names of. I picked up on a general air of light, of comfort and pleasure and curiosity. If dark magick had been worked here, I couldn't feel it.

"This is incredible," I said, walking slowly into the room. Despite the lack of windows, the room looked open and inviting. A fireplace took up one wall, and by gauging the rooms above, I figured its chimney must run through the kitchen fireplace's. Big, cozy armchairs were strewn here and there. There were closed glass cases, regular bookshelves, wooden tables piled with stacked books. Unlike Selene's personal library, this one wasn't cold or intimidating. It was all laid out neatly and beautifully organized.

"This is quite an accomplishment for someone so young," I said, wandering into the next room. I saw that it led to another room, and that there was a lavatory off to one side.

"I'm twenty-four," Justine said without artifice. "I inherited a lot of this from my mother when she moved into a smaller house. Most of what I've contributed myself are the books on the use of the stars' positions to aid or hinder magick. It's another interest of mine."

I ran my fingers lightly over books' spines, skimming titles. There were one or two books on the dark uses of magick, but that was to be expected of almost any witch's library. The vast majority of the books were legitimate and nonthreatening. Or as nonthreatening as a manual of how to make magick can be. Just about anything can be misused.

"My father would have loved this," I murmured, remembering the Da of my childhood, surrounded by books in his library at home. Candles burned down around him and still he read, late into the night. He'd often impressed on us kids how precious books were, learning was.

"Is he no longer living?" Justine asked sympathetically.

I bit back a snide retort about the definition of living and answered instead, "No, he's alive. He's at the B and B in Foxton."

"Why don't you bring him next time, then?" Justine said. "I'd be happy for him to see my library. Is he a Seeker, too?"

"No," I said, unable to suppress a quick dry laugh. "No, but he's in bad shape. My mum died at Yule, and he's taken it hard." I was surprised to hear myself confiding in her. I tend to be very closemouthed and don't often share my personal life with anyone, besides Sky and Morgan.

"Oh, how awful," Justine said. "Maybe the library will be a good distraction for him."

"Yes, maybe you're right," I said, meeting her brown eyes.

"This place is nice," I said, looking around the small restaurant. It was Monday night, and Justine had recommended the Turtledove as a likely place for Da and me to have a decent meal. Across from me, the etched lines of his face thrown into relief by the flickering firelight, Da nodded without enthusiasm. Since I had gotten back to the B and B this afternoon, he had been alternately withdrawn, confrontational, and wheedling. I figured a nice meal out would help stave off my overwhelming desire to shake him.

Not that I felt that way every second. Every once in a while, I would get a glimpse of the old da, the one I knew and recognized. It was there when he almost smiled at a joke I made, when his eyes lit with momentary interest or intelligence. It was those moments, few and far between, that had kept me going, kept me reaching out to him. Somewhere inside this bitter husk was a man I'd known as my father. I needed to reach him somehow.

"More bread?" I asked, holding out the basket. Da shook his head. He'd barely picked at his beef stew. I was going to give him another five minutes and then finish it off for him.

"Son," he said, startling me, "I appreciate what you're doing. I do. I even think you're right, most of the time. But you just can't understand what I'm going through. I've been trying and trying, but I need to talk to Fiona. I need to see her. Even if the bith dearc saps my strength or my life force. I just can't see any kind of existence where I wouldn't need your mother."

His hand shook as he reached for his wineglass, and he downed the rest of his drink. This was the most direct he'd been with me since we'd left the cabin, and it took me a moment to find my footing.

"You're right—I don't understand what it's like to lose your mùirn beatha dàn, not after you've been married and had children, made a life together," I said. "But I know that even with that tragedy, it doesn't make sense for you to kill yourself by continuing to contact the shadow world. Mum wouldn't have wanted it that way."

Da was silent, his clothes hanging on his thin frame.

"Da, do you believe that Mum loved you?"

His head jerked up, and he met my eyes.

"Of course. I know she did."

"I know she did, too," I agreed. "She loved you more

than anything on this earth. But do you think that she would be doing this if *you* had died? Or would she be doing something different?"

Da looked taken aback by my question and sat in silence for a moment.

Changing the subject, giving him time to think, I repeated Justine Courceau's offer of letting Da see her library. "It's quite amazing," I said. "I think you'd be very interested in it. Come with me tomorrow and see it."

"Maybe I will," Da muttered, tapping his fork against the tablecloth.

It wasn't a total victory, but maybe it was a step forward. I sighed and decided to let it go for the present.

On Tuesday, I called Kennet and gave him a preliminary report. I had more background checks to do on Justine and more interviewing, but so far I hadn't turned up anything of great alarm.

"No, Hunter, you misunderstand," Kennet said patiently. "Everything she's doing is of great alarm. Under no circumstances should any witch have written lists of living things' true names. Surely you see that?"

"Yes," I said, starting to feel testy. "I understand that. I agree. It's just that you made Justine sound like a power-hungry rebel, and I don't see that in her. I feel it's more a matter of education. Justine's quite intelligent and not unreasonable. I feel that she needs reeducation; she needs to be made to understand why what she's doing is wrong. Once she understands, I think she'll see the wisdom in destroying her lists."

"Hunter, she needs to be shut down," Kennet said strongly. "Her reeducation can come later. Your job is to stop her, now, by any means necessary."

I tried to keep my voice level. "I thought my job was to investigate, make a report, and then have the council make a judgment. Have you already decided this matter?"

"No, no, of course not," Kennet said, backpedaling at the implication of my words. "I just don't want you to be swayed by this witch, that's all."

"Have you known me to be easily swayed in the past, by man or woman?" I asked with deceptive mildness. Deceptive to most people, but not to Kennet. He knew me very well and could probably tell I was working hard to keep anger out of my voice.

"No, Hunter," he said, sounding calmer. "No. I'm sure we can trust your judgment in this matter. Just keep reporting back, all right?"

"Of course," I said. "That's my job." After I hung up, I sat on my twin bed for a long time, just thinking.

That afternoon I brought Daniel to Justine's cottage. As before, she was welcoming, and though I detected her shock at my father's haggard appearance, she made no mention of it.

"Come in, come in," she said. "It's gotten a little warmer, hasn't it? I think maybe spring is on its way."

Inside, Da instinctively headed for the fireplace and stood before the cheerful flames, holding out his hands. Back at the cabin, it had been as though the fire hadn't existed, so I was interested to see his reaction to this one.

"Are you warm enough, Mr. Niall?" Justine asked. "I know it can be chilly in these stone cottages."

"I'm fine, thanks," said Da, turning his back to the fire but keeping his hands behind him, toward the heat.

Justine and I talked for a while, and she told us stories about growing up with Avalen Courceau, who sounded like an intimidating figure. But Justine spoke of her with love and acceptance, and again I was impressed by her maturity and kindness. She got even Da to smile at the story of when she had built a house of cards out of some important indexed notes her mother had made. Apparently sparks had flown for days. Literally.

"Mr. Niall," said Justine, "I wonder if you could do me a favor?" She gave him a charming smile, sincere and without guile. "I don't get many opportunities to try new magick—no one around here knows I'm a witch, and I want to keep it that way. I was wondering if you would consent to be a guinea pig for a spell I've just learned."

Da looked concerned but couldn't think of any reason not to and didn't want to refuse in the face of her hospitality. "What for?"

She smiled again. "It's a healing spell."

Da shrugged. "As you wish."

"It's all right with me," I said, and she turned to give me a teasing look.

"It's not your decision," she pointed out. Feeling like an overbearing clod, I sat down on the sofa, relaxing against the plump pillows, waiting for some cat to realize I was there.

She had Da sit down in a comfortable chair, then cast a circle around it, using twelve large amethysts. She invoked the Goddess and the God and dedicated her circle to them. Then she stood behind my father and gently laid her fingertips against his temples on either side. As soon as she started on the forms and opening chants, I realized I wasn't familiar with it.

It went on for more than an hour. At different times Justine touched my father's neck, the back of his head, his forehead, the base of his throat, his temples. Da seemed patient, tired, disinterested. I myself felt almost hypnotized by the warm crackling of the fire, the deeply felt purring of the apricot-colored cat who had finally settled on me, the soothing tones of Justine's low-voiced singing and chanting.

At last I recognized the closing notes, the forms of completion, and I sat up straighter. Slowly Justine took her hands away from Da and stood back, seeming drained and peaceful. I looked at Da. He met my eyes. Was it my imagination, or was there more life in them?

He turned to find Justine. "I feel better," he said, sounding reluctant to admit it. "Thanks."

She smiled. "I hope it helped. I found it in a book I was cataloging last month, and I've been anxious to try it. Thank you for allowing me." She took a deep breath. "Now, how about some tea? I'm hungry."

Ten minutes later, watching Da tuck into his cake with the faint signs of an actual appetite, I smiled my gratitude to Justine. She smiled back. To me, this healing was one more indication that Justine was just misguided, overenthusiastic in her quest for knowledge but basically good-hearted. There was no way someone like Selene could have performed that healing rite, not without my picking up on her dark underlying motives. I'd felt none of that with Justine. She seemed genuinely what she was.

"My son told me how impressed he was with your library," Da said.

"Would you like to see it?" Justine asked naturally, and my father nodded.

I felt something like gladness inside—this was the first time he had called me his son, in front of another person, since we'd been reunited. It felt good.

12.
Trust

Today is Saturday, but I feel so incredibly bizarre that I need to come up with a whole new name for this day. "Saturday" doesn't cover it.

Last night, to take my mind off things, I agreed to go ice skating with Mary K., Aunt Eileen, and Paula at the big outdoor rink outside of Taunton. I hadn't seen Eileen and Paula in ages—I've been busy saving my grades, and they've been fixing up their new house.

It was one of the last times we could go skating—spring is coming, and soon they won't be able to maintain the outdoor ice. I felt like a little kid, lacing my skates. Mary K. bought a caramel apple. Eileen and Paula were happy and lighthearted, and all four of us were being incredibly silly and goofy. I felt happy, and I didn't think about Hunter more than about a thousand times, so that was good.

Then Paula was zipping along backward when she

lost her balance and went down hard. The back of her head slammed against the ice with a crack so loud, it sounded like a branch breaking. Immediately Eileen and I were there, and Mary K. rushed up a few seconds later.

I watched in horror as a spreading, lacy design of blood seeped across the ice.

A little crowd had gathered around, peering over our shoulders, trying to see what was happening, and Aunt Eileen rose on her knees and shooed them back. I could tell she was starting to freak out, so I took hold of one of her shoulders and told her to go call 911.

Her eyes took a second to focus on mine, then she nodded, got shakily to her feet, and skated carefully to the side of the rink.

Mary K. was trying not to cry and failing. She asked me if Paula was going to be okay.

I told her I didn't know and gritted my teeth at the amount of blood I was seeing. Paula's eyes fluttered open once, and I took her hand, patting it and calling her name. She didn't respond and closed her eyes again. I had seen that one of her pupils was tiny, like a pencil point, and one was wide open, making her iris look black. I didn't know what that meant, but I had watched TV often enough to know it was bad. Crap, I thought. Double crap.

I stroked Paula's cheek, cool beneath my hand. My hands felt so warm, even without gloves. My hands . . . a couple of weeks ago, Alisa Soto had been very ill. I had touched her, and all hell had broken loose. Did I dare try to touch Paula now? The situation with Alisa had been really weird, way different from this one. But what if I made Paula worse?

Cautiously I traced my fingers over Paula's hair, now cold and wet. I hoped no one was paying attention to what I was doing. Beneath my fingers, I felt Paula's life force pulsing unsteadily, becoming overwhelmed by a cascading flood of injuries it couldn't recover from.

I closed my eyes and concentrated. It took me a moment to orient myself, to feel my consciousness blend with Paula's. But then I was at home in her body, and I could tell what was wrong. There was bleeding inside Paula's skull. The blood on the ice was from her skin being split, but there was also bleeding inside her skull, and it was pooling at the back of her head. It was compressing her brain, which had nowhere to go. Her brain was swelling dangerously, pressing against her unmovable skull, and it was starting to shut down. Paula was going to die before the ambulance got there.

My eyes flew open at this knowledge. Eileen was white-faced, crying, trying to be brave. I saw Mary K., stroking Eileen's arm and weeping.

Very slowly and quietly, hoping no one would stop me, I closed my eyes again and rested my fingers lightly beneath Paula's head. In moments I had sunk into a deep meditation, had sent my senses into Paula again. Now I could see all the damage. Without having to search for them, ancient words came into my mind. It was a spell from Alyce, I realized. Silently I repeated them as they floated toward me, hearing their powerful, singsong melody. I pictured the pooled blood dissipating, seeping away; I thought about gently opening the collapsed veins, branching off smaller and smaller, infinitely delicate and perfect and beautiful.

As Paula's systems steadied—her breathing more even, her heart pumping more strongly, her brain returning to its preaccident state—I felt a wave of exhilaration that almost took my breath away. This was beautiful magick, perfect in its intent, powerful in its form, and gracefully expressed by the ancient voices through me. There was nothing more wonderful, more satisfying, more joyful, and I felt my heart lighten and a smile come to my face.

Then Paula's eyes fluttered open, and my happiness increased.

I sat back on my heels, exhausted, and glanced at my watch. My hand was covered with blood; I wiped it hastily on my jeans. I had done everything in three minutes. Three crucial minutes that meant the difference between life and death for someone I cared about. It was the most amazing thing that had ever happened to me, and I couldn't even take it in.

The ambulance came almost ten minutes later. Paramedics raced out onto the ice, stabilized Paula's neck and head, then moved her carefully to a stretcher. Aunt Eileen went with the stretcher, promising to call us later with news. I said I'd take her car back to my mom's house, and she could come get it later. She tossed me the keys and then ran to catch up.

After the flashing red lights had disappeared and the crowd of anxious bystanders had drifted away, Mary K. and I got stiffly to our feet. We were chilled through and bought some hot chocolate from the stand, then walked back to Aunt Eileen's car.

As I unlocked the door, I told Mary K. I thought Paula was going to be all right. She had stopped crying but still looked very upset. She got into the passenger seat without saying anything, and I looked over at her before I started the engine.

Mary K.'s large brown eyes met mine and she asked me what I had done.

I looked out the windshield into the salt-stained street—winter was ending, and it seemed like I was seeing the bare ground, bare trees, bare sidewalks for the first time. I thought of Alisa and her brief illness, how Mary K. still seemed to think I'd healed her.

I didn't know what to say.

"Nothing," I whispered.

—Morgan

On Saturday morning I finished writing my Justine Courceau report for the council. I'd spent quite a bit of time with her, discussed all the different facets of true names, had further interviews with the people in Foxton, and gone through her library. The summary of my report was that she needed reeducation but wasn't dangerous and that no serious action need be taken, once I witnessed her destroying her written list of true names.

I signed it, addressed an envelope, put the report inside, and sealed it. Da was sitting in the room's one chair. I told him what the report said, and to my surprise, he looked like he was actually listening. He rubbed his hand across his chin, and I recognized the gesture as one I make myself when I'm thinking.

"Reeducation, eh?" he said. "You think so? I mean, you think that will be enough?"

"That and destroying her list," I said. "Why wouldn't it be?"

He shrugged. "I think there's more to Justine than meets the eye."

I gave him my full attention. "Please explain."

He shrugged again. "You don't really know her. You might not want to accept her at face value."

"Do you have anything concrete or specific that should change what I said in my report?"

"No," he admitted. "Nothing more than I feel suspicious. I feel she's hiding something."

"Hmmm," I said. On the one hand, the report was written, and I didn't want to redo it, though of course I would if I turned up new information. On the other hand, Da, despite his many *enormous* faults, was still nobody's fool, and it would be stupid of me not to pay attention to what he said. On the third hand, Da had just spent eleven years on the run and was probably pretty likely to be suspicious of everyone.

"Right, well, thanks for telling me that," I said. "I'll keep that in mind this afternoon."

"Yup," Da said. "Anyway, she's got a nice library."

"Hunter! Welcome back. Come in," Justine said.

"Hello. I've wrapped up my report, and I wanted to give you the gist of it before my father and I take off." I got out of my coat and draped it over the back of the sofa, then sat down across from her.

"Oh, great. Where *is* your father?"

"Back at the B and B. He gets tired very easily, though he definitely seems better since you did the healing rite."

"I'm glad. Okay, now tell me about your frightening report on the evil and dangerous Justine Courceau."

She was openly laughing at me, and I grinned back. Not many people feel safe teasing me—Morgan and Sky are the only ones who came to mind. And now Justine.

Briefly I filled her in on what I had reported to Kennet, expecting her to be relieved and pleased. But to my surprise, her face began to look more and more concerned, then upset, then angry.

"Reeducated!" she finally burst out, her eyes glittering. "Haven't you heard a thing I've said? Have our talks meant nothing?"

"Of course I've heard what you said," I responded. "Haven't you heard what *I've* said? I thought you'd come to agree with the council's position on true names of living beings."

"I said I *understood* it," Justine cried, getting to her feet. "Not that I *agree* with it! I thought I'd made that perfectly clear."

I stood up also. "How can you not agree? How can you possibly defend keeping a written list of the true names of living beings? Don't you remember that story I told you, about the boy in my village and the fox?"

She threw her arms out to the sides. "What has that got to do with anything? That's like saying don't go to Africa because I knew someone who tripped and broke their leg there. I'm not an uneducated child!"

Before I realized it, we were shouting our views and shooting the other's down. It turned out that all week we had been dancing around each other, skirting the issues, avoiding openly confronting each other and, in so doing, had made incorrect assumptions about what we agreed on, how we felt, what we were willing to do. I had thought I was being a subtle but influential Seeker, but Justine had chosen not to be influenced.

Ten minutes into it, our faces were flushed with heat and anger, and Justine actually put out her hands and shoved against my chest, saying, "You are being so pigheaded!"

I grabbed her arms below her shoulders and resisted the temptation to shake her. "Me pigheaded? You have pigheaded written all over you! Not to mention self-centeredness!"

At that very instant, as Justine was drawing in a breath to let me have it again, I became aware that someone was watching me, scrying for me. I blinked and concentrated and knew that Justine had just picked up on it, too. It was Morgan, trying to find me. As soon as I made that connection, she winked out, as if she were only trying to locate me to see where I was. I looked down at Justine, saw what we looked like, with her hands pressed against my stomach and me holding her arms, both of us arguing passionately, and realized what it might have looked like to Morgan. "Oh, bloody hell," I muttered, dropping my hands.

"Who was that?" Justine asked, her anger, like mine, deflated.

"Bloody hell," I repeated, and without warning, my whole life came crashing down on me. I loved Morgan, but she'd been spying on me! I was a Seeker but growing increasingly uncomfortable with the council's secrecy and some of its methods. And my da! I didn't even want to go there. My father who wasn't a father; my mother who was dead. It was all too much, and I wanted to disappear up a mountainside, never to be seen again. I rubbed my hand against my face, across my jaw, feeling about forty years old and very, very tired.

"Hunter, what is it?" Justine asked in a normal voice.

I raised my head to look at her, her concerned eyes the color of oak leaves in fall, and the next thing I knew, she had pressed herself against me and was pulling my head down to kiss me. I was startled but could have pulled back. But didn't. Instead my head dipped, my arms went around her, and our mouths met with an urgency as hot as our argument had been. Details registered in my mind: that Justine was shorter and curvier than Morgan, that she was strong but less aggressive than Morgan, that she tasted like oranges and cinnamon. I drew her closer, wanting her to turn into Morgan, then realized what I was doing and pulled back.

Breathing hard, I looked down at Justine, horrified by what I had just done, even as I acknowledged that I had liked it, that it had felt good. She smiled up at me, her lips full, her eyes shining.

"I've been wanting to do that since the first moment I saw you," she said, her voice soft. "I haven't been this attracted to anyone in I don't know how long." She reached for me again and spread her hands across my chest, splaying her fingers and pressing against the muscle there. Gently I covered her hands with mine and pulled them away from me.

"Justine," I said, "I'm sorry. I don't know what to say. I shouldn't have kissed you, for several different reasons. I don't know what came over me. But I apologize."

She laughed—a light, musical sound—and tried to pull me close again. "Don't apologize," she said, her voice drawing me in without a spell. "I told you, I've been wanting to kiss you. I want you." Her eyes took on more intent, and she stepped closer to me so we were touching from chest to knees. I felt her full breasts pillow against me and the width of her hips against mine. It felt terrific, and I felt awful, guilty.

"I'm sorry, Justine," I said again, stepping back. I crossed the room with big strides and grabbed my coat. "I'm sorry. I didn't mean to hurt you." Then I was out the door like a dog turned loose and rushing toward my car.

I was back at the bed-and-breakfast hours before I had expected to be. All I wanted was to lie on my bed and figure out what the hell had just happened. I knew I loved Morgan sincerely and truly, and I knew I was intensely attracted to her. The fact that we hadn't slept together didn't seem to have any bearing on this—I was sure we would, when it was right. No, this was a freak occurrence, and I needed to figure it out so I could make sure it never happened again. I also just needed to get my head clear about the council and my father. A daunting task.

Groaning to myself, I turned my key in the lock and tried to open the door. It wouldn't budge. I tried the key a couple of times, then realized that the damned door was *spelled* from the inside! Working as quickly as I could, I dismantled all the blocking spells, then crashed into the room. Da was on the floor, hastily brushing a white substance under his bed. I lunged for it, dabbed my fingers in it, and tasted it. Salt.

"What have you been doing?" I demanded while he got up and sat on his bed, brushing off his hands. He was silent, and I looked around the room. Now I saw a small section of the concentric circles of power he had drawn on the floor with salt, and I also found a book, written in Gaelic. Written Gaelic is a struggle for me, but I could read enough to decipher that there was a chapter on creating a sort of artificial bith dearc, far from a power sink. I wanted to throw the book across the room.

"Did Justine give you this, or did you take it?" I demanded, holding the book out to him.

He looked at me. "I took it," he said without remorse.

I shook my head. "Why am I even surprised?" I asked no one. Suddenly feeling angry seemed pointless. Instead a deep sadness came over me as I accepted the fact that I wasn't enough of a reason for Da to want to live. I flopped down on my bed and looked at the ceiling. "Why am I disappointed? You don't want to stop contacting Mum. You don't care that it hurts her, that it hurts you, that it hurts me. You don't care that you're going to take away the only parent Alwyn and I have left. I just—I don't know what to do. *You* need a father, a father of your own. I'm not up to it."

"Son, you don't understand," Da began.

"So you say," I interrupted him, turning on my side, my back to him. "No one understands how you feel. No one has ever lost anyone they cared about, except you. No one has felt your kind of pain, except you. You're so bloody *special*." I didn't try to hide my bitterness. I hated the fact that I cared enough to be disappointed. I hated Da for being who he was, and who he wasn't.

"No, I mean you don't understand what I was doing," Da said, a stronger tone in his voice. "I was trying to help you."

"Help me?" I laughed dryly. "When have I ever mattered enough for you to want to help? I know I'm nothing to you. The only good thing about me is that I'm half Mum."

Silence dropped over the room like a curtain. My father was so still and quiet that I turned over to see if he was still there. He was. He was sitting on the edge of his bed, staring at me, a stunned, confused expression on his face. "You are," he whispered. "You are half Fiona. You, and Alwyn both. Fiona lives on in you."

I sighed. "Forget it, Da. I'm not going to hassle you anymore. I'm giving up."

"Wait, Hunter," he said, using my common name. "I know you won't believe this, but you, Linden, and Alwyn were the most precious things in my life, after your mother. You three were our love personified. In you I saw my strength, my stubbornness, my wall of reserve. But I also saw your mother's capacity for joy, her ability to love deeply and give freely. I had forgotten all that. Until just now."

I rolled over to face him. He looked old, beaten, but there was something about him, as if he'd been infused with new blood. I felt a more alive sense coming from him.

"I liked being a father, Gìomanach," he said, looking at his hands resting on his knees. "I know it may not have seemed like it. I didn't want to spoil you, make you soft. My job was to teach you. Your mother's job was to nurture you. But I was happy being a father. I failed Cal and left him to be poisoned by Selene. You and your brother and sister were my chance to make that up. But then I left you, too.

Not a day has gone by since then that I haven't regretted not being there to watch my children grow up, see your initiations. I missed you." He gave a short laugh. "You were a bright lad, a bulldog, like I said. You were fast to catch on, but you had a spark of fire in you. Remember that poor cat you spelled to make the other kids laugh? I was angry, you misusing magick like that. But that night, telling Fiona about it, I could hardly stop laughing. That poor cat, batting the air." Another tiny chuckle escaped, and I stared at him. Was this my father?

"Anyway," Da said. "I'm sorry, son. I'm a disappointment to you. I know that. That's bitter to me. But this seems to be where my life has brought me. This is the spell I've written."

"Maybe so, up till now," I said, sitting up and swinging my feet to the floor. "But you can change. You have that power. The spell isn't finished yet."

He shook his head once, then shrugged. "I'm sorry. I've always been sorry. But—you make me want to try." These last words were said so softly, I could hardly hear them.

"I want you to try, too, Da," I said. "That's why I'm so disappointed today." I gestured at the circles, smudged on the floor, the salt crunching underfoot.

"I really was trying to help you," he said. "I didn't trust Justine. How is she acquiring the true names of living beings? Of people?"

I frowned. "She told me she inherited some of them from her mother. Others she found by accident. Two names have been contributed by their owners, in the interest of her research."

"Maybe so," said Da, not sounding convinced. "But she also gets a lot from the shadow world."

"What?"

"I wasn't contacting Fiona this time," Da explained. "I have no wish to harm her further. But the shadow world does have its uses. One of them is that people on the other side have access to knowledge that not many can get otherwise."

"What are you talking about?" I asked, afraid of where this was going.

"Justine acquires many of the true names of living beings, including people, from sources in the shadow world," Da explained.

I blinked. "How do you know this?"

"Sources in the shadow world. Reliable sources."

I was quiet for several minutes, thinking it all through. Obviously if Da's sources were correct, I had to come up with a whole new game plan. The situation had developed a new weight, a new seriousness that would require all my skill as a Seeker. Da had gotten this information for me. He had risked his own health—not to mention the irresistible temptation of calling my mother—in order to help me in this case.

Finally I looked up. "Hmmm."

Da examined my face. "I have—a gift for you. To help you."

"Oh?"

He went to the room's small desk and took out a sheet of paper. With slow, deliberate gestures he wrote a rune in the center of the paper. Then, concentrating, he surrounded the rune with seven different symbols—an ancient form of musical notes, sigils denoting color and tone, and the odd, primitive punctuation that was used in one circumstance only. Da was writing a true name. At the end he put the symbol that identified the name as belonging to a human.

I read it, mentally transcribing it as I had been taught, hearing the tones in my mind, seeing the colors. It was a beautiful name, strong. Glancing up, I met Da's eyes.

"She is more dangerous than she seems. You may need this."

The paper in my hand felt on fire. In my life, I had known only five true names of people. One was mine, three belonged to witches whose powers I had stripped, doing my duty as a Seeker, and now this one. It was a huge, huge thing, a powerful thing. My father had done this for me.

"I have an idea," I said, feeling like I was about to throw myself into a river's racing current. "I think you need to get away from Saint Jérôme du Lac—far away. It has bad memories for you. Not only that, but Canada is too bloody cold. You need to start fresh. I think you should come back to Widow's Vale with me. Sky and I have room, and I know she'd be glad to have you. Or we could get you your own place. You could be around other witches, be back in society. You need to rejoin the living, no matter how much you don't think you want to."

For a long time Da sat looking at a blank spot on the wall. I prayed that he had heard me because I didn't think I'd be able to repeat the offer.

But at last my father's dry croak of a voice said, "Maybe you're right. I don't know how long I can resist the pull of the bith dearc. I don't want to hurt your mother anymore. I can't. But I need help."

I was amazed and wondered what I had just gotten myself into. I would have to deal with it as it came. "Right, then," I said. "We'll leave tomorrow, after I clear up a few matters with Justine Courceau." I looked again at the true name and memorized it. "We'll stop in Saint Jérôme du Lac, get what you need from the cabin, and be in Quebec City by nightfall."

My father nodded and lay down on his bed with the stiff, jerky movements of an old man.

13.
Confrontation

It isn't often that someone truly surprises me, but Hunter did this morning. First he surprised me with that ridiculous report to the council and then by running off like a scared rabbit after I kissed him. I don't understand him at all. I know he wants me, too—all week he's been looking at me like a lovesick puppy, whether he realized it or not. Did he run just because he's a Seeker and I'm the one being investigated? Granted, I'm sure there are protocols in place; I'm sure it would be frowned upon. But according to whom? The stupid council! I don't acknowledge their dominion over me, so why should they stop me from having Hunter? And I absolutely want to have him. He's so compelling, such a portrait of contrasts. He looks young but acts much older. There's a world-weary air about him, as if he's seen it all and hasn't been able to forget enough of it. And there's that intriguing scar on his neck, almost like a burn. I want to know the story behind it.

He seems reserved, but he's funny, passionate about what he believes in, a worthy adversary, and an equal. He has a deep, smoldering sensuality behind his eyes. I want to see those embers ignite. The one problem is his devotion to the council—was I just imagining it, or is that devotion wavering? Given his age, he can't have been a Seeker long. I'm sure it's not too late to show him what the council really is, how insidious they are, how poisonous. In my family alone they've stripped three women of their powers—and that's just within the last fifty years. They're threatened by anyone and anything, and they retaliate far out of proportion. If Hunter understood that, he wouldn't want any part of it.

Hunter. He'll be back. He's not the type to leave unfinished business. I want him in a way I haven't wanted a man before. I want him in my bed, in my life, in my magick. Think of it— two strong blood witches, accumulating so much pure, beautiful knowledge. And using it, only occasionally, to strike down those who have wronged us.

—J. C.

The next morning, after our last breakfast at the B and B, Da and I pulled up to Justine's stone cottage. Our bags were packed and in the boot of the car; by this afternoon Da and I would be back at his cabin, getting ready to leave for the States. I felt a strong sense of reluctance, and the true name I'd memorized seemed to burn in my mind.

This would probably be the last time I would ever see Justine Courceau. Which was fine. But I had to clear up the matter of the kiss, and more importantly, I had to witness her destroying the list of true names. Which meant first I had to convince her to do it. I had never met a witch who so openly defied the council—even Ciaran MacEwan, evil though he was, acknowledged that the council had legitimate power.

"Right, then, show time," I said, starting to open my door.

"Hunter," said my father, and I turned to look at him. "Good luck."

Encouragement from a father. I smiled. "Ta." We got out of the car.

Justine greeted my knock and gave us an easy smile. If she was upset about our kiss yesterday, she didn't show it. Today she wore a deep red sweater that made her look vital and curvaceous. I tried not to think about it.

"Bonjour," she said, letting us in. "I just poured myself some coffee. Would you care for some?"

We both agreed, and she left us in the lounge. On the floor in front of the fireplace was a large wooden crate that had been crowbarred open. I looked inside shamelessly: it was full of leather-bound books, beat-up journals, even some preserved periodicals. All about Wicca, the craft, the Seven Clans. Additions to her library.

"I see you're examining my latest shipment," Justine said cheerfully, handing us each our coffee. It was scented with cinnamon, but other than that I detected no magickal addition, no spell laid on it. I took a sip.

"Yes," I said, tasting the coffee's warm richness. "Are these about anything in particular or just general witchiana?"

She laughed her musical laugh. "Most of these are about stone magick, crystals, gems, that kind of thing. For the gem section downstairs."

"I was hoping to go downstairs again," my father said.

"Certainly," Justine said graciously. She walked Da down the hall, opened the door leading down to the library, and turned on the light. "Call if you need anything."

She came back into the lounge with an almost predatory expression on her face. "At last we're alone," she said, smiling at the cliché.

"I wanted to talk to you about yesterday," I said. I hadn't sat down and now stood before her. I put down my coffee.

"Why did you run?" she asked softly, looking up at me. She stretched out one hand and rested it against my chest. "You must know I want you. And I know that you want me."

"I'm sorry," I said. "Yesterday shouldn't have happened. It isn't just that I'm a Seeker and I'm investigating you. It's just—I find you very attractive, and I've enjoyed our times together."

"Me too," she said, moving closer. I could detect her scent, light and spicy.

"But I'm involved with someone," I pressed on.

She didn't move for a moment, then she laughed. "What does *that* mean?"

"I have a lover." All right, it was stretching the truth a bit. I *almost* had a lover. I would have, if I hadn't been such a git.

Justine's beautiful brown eyes narrowed as she weighed my words. "Where?"

"Home."

She turned away from me and walked across the room to stroke one of the cats that lay sleeping on the back of the couch. Then she dismissed my unseen lover with a shrug. "People get together," she said. "People break up. They move on. Now you've met me, and I've met you. I want you." She gazed at me clearly, and if I hadn't had the tough hide of a Seeker, I would have squirmed. "You and I would be a formidable team. We would be good together—in bed and out of it."

I shook my head, wanting to run again. I'm terrible at dealing with things like this. "Not a good idea."

"Tell me why."

"Because I have a lover. Because I'm still a Seeker and you're still someone who has an illegal list of true names. I'm here to watch you destroy them before I leave town."

She stared at me as if I had suddenly grown antlers.

I had decided not to use my secret weapon unless I needed to. Better to have her achieve true understanding. "Justine, I understand your motives for wanting to collect true names. But there's no reason for any one person to amass that kind of power, that kind of knowledge. Even though I know you're a good person and a good witch, still, power corrupts. Absolute power corrupts absolutely."

Her lip curled the slightest bit. "I've heard that before, of course," she said softly. "I didn't believe it then, either. You know, Hunter, I thought you really understood. I thought you were on my side. But you're still determined to be a council pawn."

Ignoring her dart, I held out my hands. "I'm on the side of balance. It's never a good idea to let things get out of balance, and amassing lists of true names will absolutely tip the balance."

Her face lightened, and she shrugged and looked away. "We'll simply have to agree to disagree," she said easily. "It was nice meeting you, though. How far of a drive do you have today?"

I felt that peculiar sensation of tension entering my body, my mind, my voice. It was like a gear shifting. "No, I'm afraid it isn't that simple," I said mildly. "I'm afraid I have to insist. It isn't that I don't trust you. But what would a malicious witch do with that list? What if it fell into the wrong hands? It would be much better for that knowledge to be disseminated among witches equally, or at least witches who have dedicated themselves honestly to the side of light."

I could feel her interest cool as if I were watching a fire die down. "I'm sorry," she said, her voice sounding harder, less seductive. "I just don't see it that way. So if you'll just be going, I'll continue on my life's work."

"I need to see you destroy your list," I said in a steely voice.

Justine looked at me in amazement, then threw back her head and laughed. Not a typical reaction to a Seeker's demand. Then she caught herself and looked back at me, thoughtful. "I'll tell you what," she said. "I'll destroy my list if you'll stay here and be my lover."

Well, that was an offer I didn't get every day. "I'm sorry," I said. "But that just isn't an option."

She gave me a cool smile. "Then you need to leave now, and neither of us will have gotten what we wanted."

"The list," I said.

Her anger flared, as I knew it would eventually. "Look, get the hell out of my house," she said. "You're a Seeker for the council, but you're nothing to me and have no power over me. Get out."

"Why don't you see how dangerous it is?" I snapped back in frustration. "Don't you see how impossibly tempting it is to control something just because you can?"

Something in her eyes flickered, and I thought, Struck a nerve there, didn't I?

"I'm above that kind of temptation," she spat.

"No one's above that kind of temptation," I almost shouted. "How do you get these true names, Justine? Can you look me in the eye and honestly tell me there's no dark magick involved?"

A spark ran through Justine's eyes; she hadn't known that I knew. Her mouth opened, and she seemed momentarily stunned. Just as quickly as it came, though, she recovered. "I don't know what you're talking about," she said in a low voice. "Whoever told you that, it is a lie."

"Don't waste my time, Justine." I moved closer, raising my voice. "Now destroy the list, or I'll destroy it for you!"

She flung out her hand unexpectedly, hissing a spell. Instinctively I blocked it. It wasn't major; the Wiccan equivalent of slamming a door or hanging up on me. But it was enough to make me see that I needed to up the pressure. I cringed; I had been hoping to avoid this. But it was becoming clear that Justine needed a concrete example, right before her eyes, to see a different point of view.

"Nisailtirtha," I sang softly, looking at her as I traced a sigil in the air. "Nisailtirtha." I sang her name, feeling it achieve its shape in the air between us. It was a very serious thing, what I was doing. I felt extremely uncomfortable.

Across the room Justine's eyes opened in horrified shock, and she quickly began to throw up blocking spells. All of which were useless, of course. Because I knew her true name. That was the seductive power of it.

"Nisailtirtha," I said with gentle regret. "I have you in my power, my absolute power."

She practically writhed with anger and embarrassment before me, but there was nothing she could do. I came closer to her, close enough to feel her furious, panicked vibrations, close enough to smell oranges and cinnamon and fear. "You see," I said softly, leaning close to her ear, knowing that I was eight inches taller, sixty pounds heavier: a man. "Now I can make you do anything, anything at all."

A strangled sound came from her throat, and I knew if she were free, she'd be trying to strangle me. But I held her in place with a single thought. "Do you think that's a good thing, that I have this power over you because I know your true name? Nisailtirtha? I could make you set fire to your library."

She sucked in a breath, staring at me as if a devil she didn't believe in had just materialized in front of her. A thin, stretched moaning sound came from her throat. I hated this kind of threat—of course I would never make her do anything against her will, not even destroy her list. If I did, I would have let power corrupt me. But I was willing to scare her, scare her badly. In my career as a Seeker, I had done much worse.

I said, "Now that I know your name, I could sell it. To the highest bidder. To your enemies. Everyone has enemies, Justine. Even you."

She looked like she was about to jump out of her skin. "Nisailtirtha, I could make you tell me any secret you've ever had." Tears began to roll down her face, and I knew she was about to implode from frustration and fear. She didn't know me, not really. I hated this, hated that she was being so stubborn. I went on. "Do you have any secrets, Justine? Anything you don't want me to know?"

A whimper broke free, and one hand barely clenched. "Now," I whispered, walking in back of her so she couldn't see me, "I can make you destroy your list of true names. Or I can release you, and you can choose to destroy it yourself. Which do you think would be better?"

I released the hold on her enough to allow her to speak, and she broke out in sobs. "I'll destroy it," she cried. I tried not to think about what it had been like to kiss her.

"I won't make you promise," I said, and released her. She collapsed on the couch, as if I had cut her strings. She grabbed one startled cat and held it against her chest as if to make sure I hadn't made her kill it.

"I won't make you promise because I know your true name," I said solemnly. "I have control over you—absolute, unshakable control—for the rest of your life."

Racking sobs shook her, and if I hadn't been a Seeker, I would have folded her into my arms.

"That's the danger of true names," I said. "That's the kind of control you have over everything and everyone on your list. Is that good? Are you glad I know your true name? Does it seem neutral, like pure knowledge? Or does it seem a little . . . dark?"

"*You* seem like a complete bastard," she said, still crying. Her cat was squirming to get away, but Justine held it closely, her tears wetting its fur.

"You know what? I seem like a complete bastard because I know your true name."

She had nothing to say to that.

14.
The Way Home

I hate him. He's gone now, and I'm still shaking with fury. I can't believe Hunter Niall just took my life apart. First I yell for him, hard, but couldn't get him, even with a spelled kiss. Then his insulting, asinine, pointless report to the idiot council. Reeducated! I'm more educated than any member of the council! I can't believe Hunter, who had such promise, would be so pedestrian, so shortsighted. What a disappointment—though I still held out hope that he would see my point of view. But today, oh, today I put Hunter on my list—not the list of true names, but the list of people who have wronged me and my family. He is now at the top.

How did he learn my true name? I have never written it down. How could he possibly have that knowledge? If someone told it to him, then that person knows it, too. I feel completely exposed. I don't want to move from here; this cottage is perfect. But now I know that at least two people—maybe more—know my true name. How will I ever sleep peacefully again?

My house still smells like smoke. Hunter and I performed the spell that would allow the list to be destroyed. Then I burned the list in the fireplace, crying as I watched the flames lick along its edges, making the parchment curl. It was beautiful, and I had worked so hard on it, with the gold leaf and the calligraphy. Hunter stood by, his arms across his chest, that hard chest I had felt. His face was lit by the fire, and the awful thing was that I could tell that part of him regretted destroying something so beautiful. Seeing that on his face was incredibly irritating because it only showed me again how much possibility exists within him, how close he was to being exactly what I needed him to be.

I do know this. I haven't seen the last of Hunter Niall, nor he of me. Now I have work to do.

—J. C.

I felt better once we were fifty miles away from Justine. That last scene had left me with bitter feelings, all sorts of conflicting emotions. But I was glad the list had been destroyed and glad I'd had the presence of mind to also check her computer. There wasn't much there—just a few files she had to purge. I'd have to make an addendum to my report.

Da had little to say about the whole thing—if he had an opinion, he was keeping it to himself. On the drive back to his town he seemed thoughtful, preoccupied.

In Saint Jérôme du Lac, I stopped at the liquor store and picked up several cardboard boxes. Then, back at the cabin, I helped Da pack his few belongings worth saving—some books, a wool shawl of Mum's, her notebooks and papers. He had almost no clothes; none of the furniture was fit for anything but the bin; he had no art or knickknacks. It took us barely half an hour, but even that half hour made me nervous. The longer we were there, the twitchier Da seemed to become. He kept glancing at the front door as if he would bolt. I threw his stuff into the boot of my car and hustled him out to it, leapt into my seat, and motored out of there as fast as I could without causing my entire exhaust system to fall off.

After we had been on the road for six hours, I felt calmer. Da had curled miserably in his seat, as though the act of leaving that area was physically and emotionally painful.

"We'll be stopping soon," I told him, the first words either of us had spoken in hours. "We can get a room for tonight, then tomorrow be back in Widow's Vale by late afternoon. I think you'll like it there. It's an old town, so it has some character. I'll have to call Sky and get her back from France. You'll be so surprised when you see her. Remember how she was kind of a pudge? She's quite thin and tall now."

I was chattering, completely unlike myself, trying to fill the silence. Something occurred to me, something I needed to say. "Da. I wanted to tell you. I was having a hard time with Justine back there, but knowing her true name tipped the balance. I don't know what she would have done if I hadn't been able to use it. So thanks."

Da nodded. "Once upon a time, I was a strong witch," he muttered, almost to himself. He reached down on the floor by his seat and picked up a somewhat battered, black-cloth-bound book. Its spine was unraveling, and black threads hung off it like whiskers.

"What's that?" I asked.

"I took this from Justine's library," he said.

"You *what?*" I said. "You snatched another book from her?"

"I—confiscated it," he said. "This is a memoir of the witch who first created the dark wave, back in 1682."

"You're kidding."

"It talks about the Burning Times and the War Between the Clans. . . ."

"What was his name?" I broke in, glancing away from the road to look at the book's cover again.

"Whose name?"

"The name of the witch who created the dark wave." I sighed. It was a terrible, terrible legacy—the creation of a weapon of mass destruction. Ever since that time blood witches had been living in fear. Get on the wrong side of a powerful witch who practices dark magick, and you might be the next victim of the dark wave.

Daniel opened the book and frowned. "Not a he, a she. Let me see here. Her name was—" He frowned. "Rose MacEwan."

"MacEwan," I whispered.

Like Ciaran MacEwan. Morgan's father.

"She lived in a small town in Scotland," Daniel told me. "I didn't have time to read much of it, but as the book begins, she's just a teenager."

Part of Morgan's family was from Scotland. "Do you think— is it possible that she's an ancestor of Ciaran MacEwan?"

Daniel's face clouded over. He looked over at me. "It's possible. Even likely, I suppose. Same name, same country, even." He frowned. "That would make her an ancestor also to your—Mary?"

"Morgan." Dammit, he'd barely even been listening to me.

Daniel nodded. "Not surprising." I turned to him, startled— what was he trying to say?—and he continued gravely. "To be Ciaran MacEwan's daughter—it's a dark inheritance. I wouldn't trust her so easily."

Anger flared in me. Who was he to talk about trust? I had to struggle to keep myself under control. Remember what he's been through, I kept telling myself. He's been on the run from Amyranth for eleven years. Of course he would be skittish about Ciaran . . . and anyone related to Ciaran. Once Da meets Morgan, he'll be fine, I told myself. And until then, hopefully I could keep from throttling him whenever her name was mentioned.

"But I *do* trust her, Da. I have every reason to. She's proved herself to me again and again." I glanced over at him, but I found it hard to gauge his reaction. His expression hadn't changed.

"Well, that's your decision, lad." Da's gaze turned back to the book. "In any case, Justine never should have kept such an important piece of history from the council. Who knows how useful it could be in possibly defeating the dark wave? The council should see this right away."

"Indeed they should."

On the whole, I was feeling unrealistically happy and optimistic about bringing Da home to live with me and Sky, at least until he got his own place. I pictured him six months from now, healthier, heavier, able to function around other people. If I could somehow manage to make that happen, I would feel like I had finally repaid him for the fathering he had done for the first eight years of my life. Even though I'd been without him longer than with him, still, the lessons he'd instilled in me in those years had been the basis of everything I had done since then. I was glad to have a chance to help him now.

Of course, I knew he was occasionally going to drive me stark raving mad—but I would deal with that in time.

This time tomorrow I would be seeing Morgan—I hoped. I would try to call her tonight to tell her I was on my way home. I felt bad about what she had seen when she'd scried, but I also hadn't liked her scrying for me unless she'd really needed me. On the other hand, I hadn't been able to call her much at all. So I could understand how she might have been worried about me.

And I knew I had to tell her about Justine and the kiss. I still couldn't figure out why I'd done it, and I wasn't ready to think about how Morgan would react.

I sighed. I just wanted to see her tomorrow, talk, get everything straightened out, get caught up. My chest actually ached with wanting to hold her, see her eyes, taste her lips. If she had been with me, this trip would have been so different, so much more positive. I wouldn't have felt so crazed and out of control most of the time. And nothing would have happened with Justine. . . .

Which reminded me. I had to make a decision with

regard to the council. I knew that when I got home, I'd have to have a long talk with Kennet. I was becoming increasingly uncomfortable with the council's power—and their methods—and despite whatever Justine was guilty of, I felt she'd been tried and convicted in advance of the facts.

"I'll have to call Kennet when we get home," I said to Da. I wanted to include him in my life, even confide in him. Get him used to being a father again.

"Aye? Is that who you usually deal with?"

"Yes. He was my mentor when I first decided to become a Seeker."

"He's a good man," said Da. "He tried to help with Fiona before she died."

I frowned. "What?"

"Back before Yule," Da said, looking pained again. "I knew Fiona was on the brink. I tried to tell you that time I saw you scrying for us—but we got cut off. I was devastated. In desperation, I contacted the council. Kennet sent a healer to help. We tried everything we could, but in the end, she was ready to leave."

I went very still, a deep, interior stillness. My brain started firing, and I pulled the car over to the side of the highway. It was dark, almost seven, and I left my lights on.

"What's wrong?" Da asked, peering out at the car's bonnet.

"You're saying that Kennet knew where you were, back before Yule?" I asked quietly.

"Aye."

I rubbed my chin hard, thinking. My chest felt tight, and my jaw was clenched as the truth came filtering down to me. The council had learned where my parents were three months ago. Kennet had known their whereabouts for three months!

If he'd told me, I could have come up and seen my mother while she was still alive! This knowledge stunned me. I could have seen my mother alive. I could have seen her, held her.

Kennet had known, and he hadn't told me. Why?

I thought back. Yule. Morgan and I had had the final showdown with Selene Belltower and Cal Blaire. And then we had gone to New York City, had found Killian and Ciaran MacEwan.

Could that have been it? Had the council wanted to keep me in Widow's Vale to help protect Morgan? Had they decided not to tell me, rather than give me the choice of possibly seeing my mother? Had they taken that last chance away from me?

It seemed so, I thought, swallowing hard.

If I was right, the council had treated me like a child, or a pawn. I had been manipulated, betrayed. How could they have decided my fate like that? Who were they to make that kind of decision?

Shaking, I pulled the car back onto the narrow highway. Inside, I felt as if my heart had shriveled up into a charred piece of coal. Why was I working for the council? Once I had absolutely believed in them. Did I now? I didn't know anymore. I didn't know anything. All I knew how to be was a Seeker. If I wasn't a Seeker, what would I do?

"Everything all right, son?" asked Da.

"Yes," I murmured softly.

But I was lying. Nothing was all right, nothing at all. I wondered whether anything would ever be all right again.